THE PATH OF THE EELS

The Path of the Eels

by luan starova

translated from the Macedonian
by Christina E. Kramer

AB

This is an Autumn Hill Books book
Published by Autumn Hill Books, Inc.

1138 E. Benson Court
Bloomington, Indiana 40401
USA

First Published as PATOT NA JAGULITE
© 2003 Luan Starova

This project was supported in part by an award from the National Endowment
for the Arts

NATIONAL
ENDOWMENT
FOR THE ARTS

Cover design and layout by Justin Angeles

Autumn Hill Books ISBN: 9780998740003
Library of Congress Control Number: 2017934240

www.autumnhillbooks.org

The Eel

BY EUGENIO MONTALE

TRANSLATED FROM THE ITALIAN BY MILLICENT BELL

The eel, the siren
of freezing oceans, who leaves the Baltic
to reach our seas,
our estuaries, the rivers
that she climbs again, deep under opposing tides
of branch narrowing into more slender branch, and then
in the root fibers of streams piercing
always closer to the rock's heart,
filtering like bright water through
rivulets of mere mud until one day
light flashed from chestnut leaves
lights up the quiver in a dead pool,
in runnels that slant down
from the ridges of the Apennine to the Romagna;
the eel, torch, whip,
Love's arrow on earth
which only our stagnant ditches or the dried
streams of the Pyrenees lead back
to paradises of fecundity;
the green spirit who seeks
life there only
where drought and desolation gnaw,
the spark that says
everything begins where everything seems
charcoal, a burnt-down stump;

brief rainbow, iris, twin
to the glance mounted within your lashes
which you keep sparkling and untouched
in the midst of the sons
of Man, all sunk in your mire — Can you
not see she's your sister?

Chapter 1

I stood on the edge of a great cliff that perched like a balcony above the blue eternity of the lake. Behind me, in Macedonia, stood the Monastery of St. Naum. A proud peacock strutting along its red-tiled roof added to the beauty of this holy landscape. My gaze crossed the border marked by an invisible buoy that divided the two countries and reached the nearby shore of Albania.

My eyes settled on my hometown, Pogradec, the starting point of our family's final exodus in that far-off year of 1942, after which we were condemned to a land of no return. If one followed the course of Mother's memories, along the ring of keys belonging to houses abandoned by our family's ancestors, the oldest key belonged to a house on the shores of the Ionian Sea, whose waters lap our native land. The house was at least several centuries old. Also hanging from Mother's ring of keys were keys belonging to old houses that had disappeared at the time of the great family schism many centuries ago. Here Mother's recollections ended, and Father's began, through his struggle to probe ever deeper into our family's secrets.

For years I searched Father's books and notes for the starting point of our family's exodus through the Babel that is the Balkans. I dug deeper into Father's unfinished project — his attempt to find salvation from Balkan history by studying the collapse of its empires, a history through which our family history was dragged as well — a project now reduced to a pile of papers, yellowed and eaten by time, its meaning faded.

Father was deeply engaged in a study of the history of the Ottomans in the Balkans and the consequences of that history on the fate of our family. For him, the unsolved family riddle remained: What had happened during the past five centuries of Ottoman rule in the Balkans and how, after its defeat, did the family schism occur, the change of faith, the splintering of its descendents? How, after the Ottoman siege and victory, had one branch of our relatives risked life to cross to the other seashore with its old faith intact, carrying the obligatory ring of keys for unlocking houses now aflame along with a rescued icon or two or holy book in hand, while the other part of that same family, of which I, too, was a distant descendant, remained by the seashore for many generations — as if for all eternity — calling out to its kin on the other shore, hoping fate would one day bring them close again? And so one part of our family remained closer to Europe, the other to Asia.

Centuries passed; our family lost all hope that it would one day be united. It was difficult to say which branch suffered greater adversity: those who had continued with the same God or those who had, either by force or free will, converted. In the Balkans, after putting up resistance, one always paid the price of defeat, almost to the brink of extinction. At first, no one would grasp the hand of the victor. But as one of my ancestors said, "If you can't bite the hand, kiss it." And so it transpired that our family found itself with a new God and new, unimagined temptations. Some accepted the new faith; others rejected it. Either way, the course of the family's destiny was altered. An order came from Constantinople that the family would be separated from the sea and would have to seek a new destiny elsewhere…

Reluctantly, and with great trepidation, our ancestors undertook the family's first resettlement. For the first time in centuries, they abandoned their houses by the sea.

Our family's dream between the two seashores was cut short. Only family legends remained that recalled its glorious past. Hidden in the deepest roots of memory was the polyphonic song of victory and defeat, unrest and compromise, never resolved, never completed. Yet its messages survived, so that someday one of the descendants could interpret it at last. Our ancestors sent petitions all the way to Constantinople begging to be settled by water's edge, either on the banks of a river or the shore of a lake.

As compensation, they were granted houses and lands by the shore of this lake, right there at the edge of the small town on which I stood gazing from the high ridge by the monastery, peering through the old spyglass that Father once brought from Constantinople and through which three generations have peered at their native land across the border. They arrived with a new faith, but still retained some traces of the old. For many in the family, that monastery remained a holy place of their lost faith. Our ancestors were, then, caught between two faiths, one not fully uprooted, the other not fully implanted. This situation seemed to make them more tolerant, less radical in their relations with each other, and in their relation to other faiths.

The monastery was a temple of balance between the Christian and Muslim populations. Its patron saint was a savior, a healer of pain, and a banisher of evil for all people of good will regardless of their faith. Our ancestors remained tied to the monastery, despite their new faith, even taking part in its defense at times when intruders threatened.

One could freely say that every way in which history clouded the waters and the souls of the people — frequent waves of brutality, victories and defeats of empires, attacks and manipulations of ideologues, and the unknown consequences of conversion — the lake, with its magical renewing clarity, would wash clean, brightening hope even at the darkest hour.

Many years had passed since my last visit to the monastery. At that time, my mother was still alive. She still maintained the family equilibrium that had been established when Father was alive. She endured, the last pillar of the family. I have a clear memory of her lighting a last candle in the monastery, directing her gaze to her hometown on the shore across that impenetrable — but invisible — border. Her gaze rested on our former house — a house that had been confiscated — whose keys dangled from the inherited family ring.

But Mother was no longer alive. It was my fate to be left alone there by the lake, on the monastery heights. Hovering between land and sky. Like the families in Chagall's paintings, more in the sky than on the ground.

After Mother died, my older brothers, born in that lakeshore town, disappeared without ever returning to the town that was just within their reach. For a moment, the lake seemed to me a giant pool of tears.

This thought, in which consciousness and unconsciousness merged, transported me to a silent blue dream that merged with the lake's blueness and solitude. I was dreaming my waking — perhaps I was awake — when I heard Mother's quiet voice, a voice present within me since the first moments of my life:

"Son, my dearest son, don't look into the blueness. It will bewitch you and carry you down to the bottom of the lake!"

In my dream and in my daydream, I stared into the lake's blue depths. I turned. There was no one there. I looked toward the monastery. The peacock spread its wings; it looked as if a rainbow appeared above its proud head.

I turned toward the lake. I felt even more alone in this blue eternity. It had been years since Mother had vanished, vanished even from my dreams. Now she was with me. More present than ever.

I spent the night at the monastery. I hoped that some of my loved ones would come to me in my dream. But I could not shut my eyes.

At dawn, I approached the nearby Macedonian–Albanian border. The watchtower was several yards away. I had not entered my native Albania since that fateful year of 1979, when it was the only place in the world to celebrate the centennial of Stalin's birth. Now, in 1997, I entered at the new border crossing by the monastery; modern buildings had been erected at the borders of these neighboring countries in the spirit of hope that this new era would bring them closer.

It was as if a new hurricane had struck my native Albania. After the belated fall of the Stalinist dictatorship and Albania's desire to catch up with the rhythm of this new era in one breath, after the catharsis of internal reckoning and revenge and the opening of a country that had been sealed for half a century, history rushed on as never before.

People were busy leaving their native land at any cost. They stormed the boats in the harbors to cross the sea to reach Western Europe and beyond across the oceans. They crossed borders high in the mountains; with their final strength and last hope, they pressed onward day and night. They fled; alone, they fled from their own kin, from themselves; they raced forward without looking where they were going, simply to flee their native land.

It was an epidemic, a curse. It was as if I were the only one returning. I was returning to my native land to see what had happened to my extended family still living there in this new time of freedom and democracy. And I, like my father before me — like all of our family in exile — was following my paradoxical fate. Everyone was fleeing. I returned.

Among the closest of Father's kin, all that remained was his youngest sister, already well into her life's ninth decade. She was dressed all in black, her face hard. It was her eyes alone that emitted that familiar energy, goodness, and quiet strength, the source of our perseverance during our long Balkan exile. A whole family had grown up around her: sons and daughters-in-law, daughters and sons-in-law, grandchildren. But each of them had their destination, somewhere else to go without return: some to Australia or New Zealand, the luckier ones to America.

Why had those not been the destinations for Father's family when it had crossed the border? How little had changed in the family's history on both sides of the border!

My father's sister, despite the heavy blows of fate she had suffered, stood upright, and cheerfully greeted me at the doorway to her home. Through tears, she was first to speak.

"I have been waiting for you to come," she said. "I dreamt of you yesterday. You were high up on the great cliff above the deep water. I said to you: "Don't look into the blue waters of the lake. It will bewitch you and carry you off.""

A shiver ran through my body. I could not calm myself in the teary embrace of my father's sister. How could the dreams of my dead mother and Father's living sister combine in my sleep? Who could believe one's fate? Do people's dreams separate and merge when a border — a simple border-line — divides them, a line dreamt up and drawn by people from another era?

My aunt noticed my agitation. She grew calm. A few final large tears rolled down her cheeks. She was just as she had been when she last visited us — she had been allowed to cross the border solely for family burials. Anyone who could survive those tough times had to have spirit, though her heart was always tested. Still, her heart would hold out until her last nephew was settled. She knew her fate. In the end, she would be left alone by the lake, enveloped in the silent cry of all her kin who had departed; she would become their living beacon of hope.

I searched for the right words. I sat in the middle of the *minder*, in the spot reserved, by custom, for important guests. People came to see me, people I had never seen but who were my close relatives. Others peered down from their photos on the walls from far-off Australia, America, and far-ther-off New Zealand, captured forever behind glass like pinned butterflies, like an herbarium of lost illusions.

My father's sister recounted times past. She had lived with her sons and daughters in their own house as if they were tenants. Following the collapse of the Stalinist system, the borders opened, and some injustices were some-what rectified, but their house was not restored to them — they were assigned an apartment here, in Kalevo. If one of the grandsons had not gone to the minister, this wrong, too, would not have been righted. Soon after, the Socialists came to power, and someone took a fancy to my aunt's apartment.

Someone else from the Socialist government declared that the old woman had suffered enough and should be left in peace. She should be allowed to return to her home. And so it was.

The house came alive as relatives both close and distant welcomed me. Though the border had been open awhile, we had somehow been riveted to our places. The past had made us unaccustomed to hope.

I was embraced by close relatives whom I did not know, relatives who had never seen me before. I watched Father's sister quietly talking. I recognized the blue expressiveness of Father's eyes, the search for warm words that always lifted one's mood. Then, suddenly, she stood and began to speak.

"Surely God has sent you to us at this time. It is true He has not done a lot for us, yet he has not abandoned us forever. I will live a bit longer, until the last child leaves for Australia. That is what is written. And there is no escaping what is written."

Immediately, I wanted to delve into the old woman's way of thinking, her fatalism, as she expressed the power of fate and her resignation when there was no strength left to resist. I had encountered this spirit in our branch of the family, too, and had often been disgusted by it, but the inertia stemming from an inherited respect for our patriarchal traditions, had made me adopt it as a sort of compromise. I did not have strength even now to oppose it in my aunt. She seemed to sense my disquiet and continued.

"Your father, may he rest in peace, left just in time," she said. "You saw other torments. You did not see the torments we endured here. The cursed time of Stalinism, followed by the Chinese. They pitted us one against the other. That's been the rule forever since time immemorial here in our Balkans. We become our own worst enemies. They took away our fields and our houses and plowed up the graves of our ancestors."

Something deep inside me started when my old aunt mentioned plowed-up graves. Here, in my family's native land — the native land of the heroes of my Balkan saga — the main avenue of my search was closed.

I thought first of the grave of my father's mother, unquestionably the central figure in the family saga, the one I sought most in my quest.

"What happened to grandmother when she died?" I asked. "Where is she buried? Was hers among the plowed-up graves?"

"Ah, poor thing, she was lucky in her death at least. She died immediately after the war. Hers was the only grave that survived intact; she was the only one God did not forget."

My aunt sensed my emotions when she mentioned that her mother's grave was still intact. She was also moved. I had only the vaguest memories of my Turkish grandmother, whom I had last seen fifty years ago when she crossed the border on her last trip to Constantinople. She taught me some Turkish, a few words, of which I always remembered the phrase *aç kapı*: open the door! Within me, there remained forever the opened door that my Turkish grandmother left to me in my exile, the door of her great, unfinished dreams to go out into the world, to escape the Balkans.

In those fifty years since my grandmother's death, a half-century's absence, the significance of this woman in my search to understand Father's Balkan exile was interwoven with my consciousness, and grew to mythic proportions.

And now, I had perhaps reached the moment of truth as I followed the life of this strong Balkan woman. My aunt, as if following the course of my inner thought, continued with animation.

"My mother was of Turkish descent," she said. "God granted me a whole half-century to live with her. She was a strong woman. She lived several lives in one, helping all of us. Her soul — a soul torn by all the separations and departures — could contain all our sufferings."

My aunt was visibly stirred. Her older daughter handed her a glass of water and medicine, likely for her heart, to calm her down. But telling her nephew about her mother both excited her and calmed her. Gathering her strength, she continued.

"I don't know, my son, which of her pains to tell you about. I couldn't begin to tell you all of them. She had such a great soul; her maternal feeling provided the family strong roots, which grew through her boundless and patient love.

"This cursed life. Our cursed fate. Her relatives were descendants of a renowned qadi's family. They lived for centuries in Prilep. Her father was a renowned qadi as well. He was the first in generations to sense the end of the empire. He decided to uproot the whole family, abandon all their lands and houses, and follow his fated path to Constantinople. He felt that his uprooted family could take root there once again. Despite everything, he couldn't uproot hope as well.

"He was a powerful qadi, who left behind a great deal, but who also took much away for his new life in Constantinople, in the unfolding of events that he foresaw. Still, every summer he would return to his native city by the lake. He quickly became friends with our family, my father in particular, who was by that time a lonely widower. Your grandfather was a strong man, but he had been broken by the early death of his first wife and the torments of his new life with the children, who, even though they had reached adulthood, were now motherless.

"Huge family quarrels began that have not yet been resolved, mainly about how to divide the land. No matter how you divide it, it is impossible to please everybody. After he divided what he had to divide and found some peace, he was consumed by a new worry. All his closest kin, on both his mother and father's sides, left for Constantinople. They left in time to get themselves well settled. And they succeeded, wonderfully. They ended up in palaces, but forgetfulness took its course. No force on earth could separate your grandfather from the lake. He stayed behind in his loneliness beside the shore, holding the great spyglass your father had brought him from Constantinople. He was left behind to watch over the bitterly divided root of the family on its native soil beside the great expanse of water..."

My aunt seemed to follow the inner line of my curiosity about our divided time, and she continued.

"One evening before his departure, while gazing out across the blue expanse of the lake, the old Prilep qadi poured out the depths of his soul to my father over a glass of rakija. 'My dear friend, I have come to bid farewell both to you and the lake. I am taking my whole family to Constantinople. Our family's time in the Balkans has come to an end. We were citizens of a strong empire that ruled five hundred years. But our time has now passed forever. We have not become part of Europe, nor have we freed ourselves from Asia. We need to leave for Constantinople before we are driven there by force and humiliation. History does not forgive if you don't follow its course wisely; you have to flow with it, not ahead of it or behind it. We are leaving behind the graves of our ancestors here in the Balkans.'

"That's how the qadi spoke to my father. He poured out his soul to the very dregs. As the light on the opposite shore faded, the qadi told my father the secret he had been carrying deep inside for a long time: 'My dear friend, for years I have been coming to this lake and enjoying the hospitality of your home. I have always considered you a close friend. And I deeply respect your family. Of all those we leave behind, you are the one we will miss the most. I am taking with me five daughters and four sons. They are all ready for our great journey. They will undoubtedly handle the uncertainties of the future better than I will. I see you here a young man, but already a widower with your life still ahead of you. It is not from some long-standing tradition for a father to offer a daughter in marriage, but I leave my youngest daughter to be your wife. Believe me, my friend, it is as though I hear the voice of providence telling me to do this. Let my daughter be a bridge between our families.'

"Father accepted the hand of the qadi's daughter with joy and good fortune. My son, new Turkish blood now flowed into our family; our fate was quickening. Son, it would take a whole century to tell you about this Turkish mother, an orphan of sorts, the strong source of life that raised Father's family … "

My aunt fell silent. She must have wanted the conversation to take a different turn. Time was pressing. I had to return that evening to the other shore of the lake.

She went to search through a large bag for a photograph of her mother, and my thoughts filled with impressions of the woman who had such an uncertain and difficult fate and had such strength to endure it. Who was this woman who would so strongly determine Father's later path, the path of the family? In her life, the family's fate was most present.

My aunt was pleased to find a photograph of her mother. For the first time in a half-century I saw her face: an old woman with a stern expression, broad brow, dark eyebrows. Beside her sits her husband, visibly older, thin, with sunken cheeks, a fierce expression, holding his pipe with authority. Here is my father, likely in his thirties, tall, fit, with a smart moustache, and beside him my slender mother. Near them are the younger children.

This journey through family photographs lasted a long time; it was as if we were journeying through a labyrinth of our family's past Balkan time, through this herbarium of a vanished life, left for me to search. For the first time, I gazed into many faces that — my aunt told me — were my close relatives.

My aunt brought new photos. We had lost all sense of time. The hour of parting was approaching. She wanted me to stay longer, sensing that this would be our last meeting. I assured her I would come again. She escorted me to the doorway and embraced me warmly. She was my closest living relative from the generation of my father's family on both sides of the border.

Chapter 2

At sunset, I crossed the border from the Albanian side. I returned to the monastery. The sun, a red-blue tear, was sinking down in the most beautiful sunset I can recall on this earth. In the fading light, I could make out the contours of my hometown, which seemed more absent now than ever before. Just a few hours ago I had been there, and now it was as if I were looking at a completely different city.

I stopped, pensive, beside the monastery well; a hundred meters at its bottom, it joins the lake. I peered deep into the well as if our family's vanished time had collected there. Reflected in the depths was the broken surface of the lake's waters.

From the bottom, I could hear the whisper of the lake's waves breaking, the breathing of the saints. I set off toward the path that sloped down the rocky ridge on which the monastery perched, toward the largest lake spring, which connects the two countries and ends in the roiling river that runs into the lake.

The waters rushed from all sides, churning, but clear, foamy, pouring into the lake, a veritable moving celebration. I stopped on the shore by the blue of the river basin. The spring waters spilled noisily into the lake. They were like the flowing roots of the lake, the very life within it that began more than two million years ago.

I peered absent-mindedly into the strong white-blue current, which seemed to spread into the lake like a rainbow of light. My mother's voice was not there to warn me that the lake's attraction could pull me into its depths. The waters called out for me to follow their current, to travel with them across the lake. To cross the nearby border marked somewhere beneath.

From my subconscious, a voice welled up with growing intensity, a voice whose source I could not ascertain: perhaps it arose from life, from the strong family signs imprinted on this terrain, or from the truths in Father's books that had continuously layered in my consciousness, or from my search across this region.

I could not, in fact, determine whether I was being summoned by Father or by the books he had read in an order established by his alchemistic quest through his library, as he embarked on one of his great unrealized circular travels through the waters that circumnavigate the planet.

It was evident that this was the start of the great migration path of the eels that led across the lake, traversing the river that flowed beneath, then across the seas, out to the ocean and, through their descendants, back again. According to Father's thinking, the family could escape from the cursed cycle of exile only by faithfully following the path of the eels.

I watched, entranced, as the white-blue and deep blue foamy waters of the lake and river crashed against one another, sparkling with the light of thousands of crushed pearls.

"Son, be careful, they will bewitch you, they will carry you off into the waters. Either flee or follow the path of the eels."

Surely that was Father's familiar voice, as if returned from death to this place filled with the ecstasy of nature. I was at the exact location where, according to Father's earlier assumptions, the path of the eels — the family's path in exile — began and ended. This was why my sense of Father's presence grew with such intensity, emerging from my subconscious.

The message — evoked in this region where spirituality poured forth from the waters — was clear: I must follow the uncertain path of the eels and join Father's quest to seek the reasons for, and the significance of, his great Balkan dream to find an exit from the Balkans for our family.

One had to seek out the meaning of the books in his library, their order and relationship to the other books; one had to search through one labyrinth to find an exit or entry into another labyrinth, to live with the comfort of the quest itself, to find calm at the crossways of the Balkan labyrinths.

Surely, Father's search along the mysterious migratory route of the eels, along the waterways of our planet, had broader significance for his discovery of a congruity between the pathway of the eels and the pathways of people.

I turned my gaze again to the rapid waters flowing into the lake. They marked the main artery that flowed out to the spring. In these restless waters countless eels hid. These watery queens from the depths of the lake's waters, with their distinct migratory fate, are, according to ancient Far Eastern beliefs, God's heralds.

The strong current flowed past, evoking a sense of transience. According to Father's conjectures, here in these thick blue waters began the great path of the eels that the family must follow in its search for an exit from the Balkans.

The eels, princes of the lake's depths, were completely invisible, but their presence and departure permeated the landscape. Right here, at the eels' point of departure from the lake across the waterways of the planet, Father's great utopian dream was born for the family to follow the path of the eels to America, and then, through its descendants, to return.

Father's library contained every conceivable sort of document — maps, drawings of eels, books about eels written in various alphabets — and marked out on the globe he had brought from Constantinople was the path of the eels with miniature models of the lake, the river to the sea, the path to the Sargasso Sea, and back again.

Both in Father's library and in the life of the family, the path of the eels, along with any thought of following it to America and back, had come to an end and been forgotten — one more of Father's many dreams in his exile.

It was left to me to search the imaginary path preserved in Father's books. In moments when my thoughts were at an impasse, I turned my gaze toward the lake's broad expanse. Again, the lake appeared to me as a giant teardrop, a tear without borders. My soul had never felt so parched.

The lake remained our great source of hope. In these waters, through their blue labyrinth, one could touch the silence, laden with meaning, of our ancestors hidden in the waves; the breath of saints, captured at the bottom of the well; the very lake beside the Monastery. Entranced, I looked at the lake, just as Father had on one of his returns to the Balkans. The lake had its natural austerity. I had been left the task of determining my part in the vicious cycle of the family dilemma: to remain or follow the path of departure. The lake waters had never seemed so crystalline to me.

The bottom, the very roots of the lake, could clearly be seen. A bright greenness reigned. At that moment, there could be no better mirror in which to see reflected people's lives, the life of the family. Was it better to remain beside this lake or to go? Was it better to yield to the fugue of an unknown exile?

My mother wanted us to hold on to our roots beside the lake; Father wanted us to uproot ourselves, to go — it did not matter whether to the West or the East, to Europe or Asia. Destiny knows its own path; such was the family's destiny in exile. These two possible streams were continuously interwoven in the family labyrinth.

At one period, Father began an intensive study of the migratory patterns in the life cycle of the lake's birds, fish, and insects. He was fascinated by their happy departure and return. Why couldn't people also become accustomed to these happy migrations?

This was the reason Father became so deeply absorbed in his search for the path of the eels. The circular planetary journey of the eels across the waterways, shared by generations, represented a model in nature that Father wished to adapt to his understanding of the family's circular movement on a path from the lake, across the river and the sea, across the ocean and back again, at a time when Stalinist Communism still threatened the Balkans.

Studying the harmonious path of the eels, a path older than man's existence, Father faced the truth: his path had diverged from nature's true course. As part of the family legacy, I was left to interpret Father's search for the path of the eels, a model passed to me, in all its reality and mysticism, an affirmation of that time in which he knew he would not find it. I was left to interpret this great Balkan illusion, as though carried along by some quixotic impulse.

As an inheritance, my father's laboratory of great Balkan ideas — the library he brought into exile — was left to me with all its secrets, with Father's spirit held in the pages of his books, which were to be read and interpreted in the order in which they had been left.

We always settled beside bodies of water and were condemned to dream a great and never-ending dream of departure, as well as an unrealized dream of joyous return. In reality, we knew that whoever crossed that cursed border lost forever the chance of return.

We never would reach our enduring fatherland; it would always evade us, in rapid motion, but always out of reach. Our migrations always began from the lake; we would give ourselves over to the rivers, the seas, the ocean, always hoping to return. We truly found ourselves forever at crossroads in a labyrinth of waterways. Anonymous waters seemed to carry in their currents all our family secrets, and also the secret of the path of the eels.

The eels pointed out a path for the family's destiny, like an arrow in the great compass of its existence. My father sought every possible proof to convince himself and his family that there was no other way out.

Father concealed a hope that the eels would point to a way out of the Balkan labyrinth. The river always led somewhere else, to others lands, a symbol of otherness. Father was certain that the eels carried our family's great dream to the shores of the American continent together with an unspecified code that would lead to our return.

Chapter 3

It was the early decades of the 20th century, and Father had just returned from Constantinople. For many intellectuals in the first years after the fall of the Ottoman Empire, returning to the Balkans was a return path back to fatalism, against the tide of fate. With difficulty Father adjusted to life in his hometown by the lake. Given the books he had brought home with him, he easily became a target of government suspicion. He became even more suspect when Italian forces occupied the town.

His mother, of Turkish roots, wanted to leave with her newly founded branch of the family to join the old branch already well established in Constantinople, but her husband did not want to leave. Her gene that wished to go competed with her husband's that wished to stay. We children would later experience this same dilemma: to go or to stay. We were constantly faced with this great conundrum: how to escape the vicious Balkan cycle.

In those moments when life was most difficult, my father, following a habit inherited from his father, would walk to the edge of the lake near the most rapid spring water, the spot where he imagined the path of the eels began. Here his thoughts would quicken their pace. They led inexorably to departure. He could sense his and his family's coming migration. He stood there entranced by the rapid spring waters near the old family home. He was transfixed by the flow of the waters. A well-known voice interrupted his reverie:

"Son, don't look down into the waters; they will bewitch you and carry you along with them!"

It was his father's voice. He turned; their eyes met.

"Father!"

"Son, what is tormenting you?"

"The thought of departure!"

"By what route, son?"

"God only knows!"

"Across the lake is a different country, different people. Son, if you don't live with your own people, with whom are you going to live?"

The old man had changed his strategy for leaving. All his brothers and sisters had moved to Constantinople when the Ottoman Empire was still strong. They gave up their land holdings beside the lake and exchanged them for new ones in Constantinople; they slipped into the upper echelons of the Constantinopolitan hierarchy. They occupied good positions.

But the old man had remained in the Balkans to maintain the house beside the lake and face the raging waves, to defy his family history. His heart was crushed by strong waves of sadness and nostalgia. His son, after a moment, answered him:

"Father, there is talk of even more difficult times. The Balkans will suffer the most. This is a century of wars. We must follow our family while there is still time!"

"My life passed under Turkish rule. We did not witness great wars. We somehow became unused to them. And war never continued inside us, deep within us."

Pensively, staring out into the depths of the lake, my father listened. The old man continued.

"No matter what path you set out on, son, you will never find the peace you have in your own country, neither in this life or the next. Son, if you leave, know that there is no return. And were God to grant you return, you would arrive in some other era. Your true time would escape you. Yet if you remain in foreign lands and die there, foreign soil will never absorb your bones and your soul will never find its celestial way."

The old man stated this final advice. Father said nothing. He did not want to contradict him, even though departure was in his thoughts. He continued to gaze into the translucent water that spread out across the lake's expanse.

"Son, don't look into the blueness. It will bewitch you!" the old man repeated.

Father's gaze persisted, fixed on the flowing waters.

"What are you staring at, son?" the old man interrupted his thoughts.

"Father, this is where the path of the eels begins."

"The path of the eels?" the old man was surprised.

"Yes, the path of the eels."

"What kind of path is that, son, which path? Have those damned books in the attic tricked you? Your mother worried that those books about eels may have addled your brain."

"The eels, Father, leave from these springs. They travel with thousands of others to the place where the waters exit the lake, and then, once across the river, they reach the sea and swim out into the ocean, the Atlantic Ocean. They reach the shores of America, and their descendants return along the same path."

"Son, do not get mixed up in God's business!"

"This isn't God's business! This is what science tells us!"

"Well, son, what do science and the path of the eels have to do with us?"

"They have a lot to do with us, Father. These hidden eels mark out our exit route. They mark the end of borders."

"Son, you put too much faith in your books. They will bewitch you just as these waters do now!"

"If nature can protect them on their journey around the world, why shouldn't man accompany them on their path? To discover new happiness. To flee the ill fortunes of the Balkans!"

"Son, you are intelligent and well read. You have returned from Constantinople with a qadi's diploma. The people trust you. Both Muslims and Christians. They respect you. Why would you set off along that path and follow, as you say, those cursed eels?"

"Father, there is talk of difficult times. Fascism is at the door. They will set us against each other once again. They are already pointing fingers at me. If I am not with them, I must be against them."

"Who told you that?"

"Our people, our own blood!"

"Don't listen to what they say. I'll straighten things out with them. They're still angry. When I remarried, there were many unresolved disagreements about how to divide the land. But son, that is no reason for you to leave. It is not up to us. Some family has left. I stayed. So did you. God helps those who remain in their native land more than those who leave. Seven years in a cursed foreign land, and not even the dog greets those who departed. Leaving is dying, son, with little hope of survival; stay with your first life!"

Not much time passed before the old man faded away beside the lake. He disappeared forever. My father never forgot his words. The family burden had been passed on to him. He had to make the decision to leave or to stay. But his mother was also there. Now, having lost the main pillar of her family, she began to think more often about setting off after her relatives in far-off Turkey. Foremost in her thoughts was her Constantinopolitan dream: to catch up with her own people and join them. The poor thing wanted to weave a new nest there for her children among her people.

Before the war, she had traveled to Constantinople. She went to Izmir, the first stage in the family exile. Then to Iskidar. But time had done its work. She could not even take hold of the little bits of inheritance her father had left her. She was a stranger in her own land.

Her sisters wondered at her old archaic Turkish. It was, after all, Ottoman Turkish, her mother tongue in which Turkish, Arabic, and Persian mixed together, sifted through the linguistic sieve of her time. There were words her sisters spoke that she could not understand at all, and words of hers that were incomprehensible to them.

Before she left, she went to visit her father's grave. She shed a century's worth of tears, sufficient for all the years they were separated, tears as bitter as her fate. She returned to the Balkans, broken.

Father had waited for her there on the shore where all the family's travels to Constantinople began and ended. They embraced. Father felt her sadness and the tears on her cheeks. It was clear to him and the whole family that an invisible border now stood on the path to Constantinople.

His old mother, now broken, was left with her two sons: Father with his lost hope of returning to Constantinople, the other with lost hope of departing for London. Just like their father, she could not prevent them from leaving.

She gathered them together one evening and gave them her final words of advice.

"Your mother was unable to find a place for you in Constantinople," she said. "Times there are different now; our people are no longer our own. We have no haven there. There is no haven for us or our hopes. I am powerless and now too old to leave. I will stay in our house by the lake. That is what your father asked of me, and it is also what my soul tells me. But you go where the Lord shows you your path. There is a war coming. We will survive it. What haven't we survived? You will return."

My father then turned to his brother.

"Should we go east?" he asked. "We will be closer to our relatives who went to Constantinople."

"Since I didn't stay in London and I did not start a family, I will stay here forever," his younger brother answered. "I will not leave again. There is no third route; my place is here."

"Hard times are coming, my brother. Fascism is going to ignite the Balkans. We have to get out in time. Along with mother and the others."

"I am staying here. I have not done anything wrong to anyone!"

Their mother wisely said nothing. She could not judge one way or another.

"Fascism is looming," Father continued. "Everything will be blinded by it and damned. We have no other way out. Let's leave across the lake! Different country, different fate. But if you are not going to leave, Brother, let our mother be shared between our families."

That is what they agreed. That same night, Father confided his plan of departure to our family and to his oldest and dearest friend, Guri Poradeci. We were not from the same family and faith as he was, but our ancestors had mixed their blood and become blood brothers; no force on Earth could separate us; we were more than family. During the night, our friend spirited us across the border, across the lake, in the family boat we had inherited long ago.

Father took his most important documents and books, whichever would be needed by the great seafarer for his grand, uncertain crossing of the Balkan Ocean. He carried the manuscript of his life's project: *The History of the Balkans through the Collapse of Its Empires*. We carried the holy books and several documents related to the East and the West as well as books about eels.

Chapter 4

Father wanted us to set off from the clear spring whose water flows into the lake, waters that resemble a ridgeline cutting a path across the unseen border, a border that has been continuously drawn and redrawn. Here, one could trace the true path of the eels, the most beautiful and most uncertain pathway on Earth. That bright living line across the blue lake was like a shadow of Halley's comet, which had appeared just once during the lifetime of Father and his family.

Mother carried the ring of keys to our shuttered houses, as well as the key to our former house by the sea, which now was surely in ruins. This was our fate — to carry the keys of our ruined houses where only hope of return was locked inside.

She was the only one who shared and suffered the consequences of Father's illusions. In the depths of her being, she never ceased understanding and loving her husband, sharing with him even their last hope of escape.

With sensitivity and respect, Mother internalized the most hidden of Father's fears; she expanded them, adding meaning she herself sensed; it was as if father's self flowed into hers. There was an intangible thread, a hidden bridge that allowed exchange from one to the other. That thread was their love that gave them more strength to support their family.

Now Father had his pursuit of the eels, which Mother, knowing this was another of Father's illusions, understood and bore the weight of. It seemed as if there were no fate more bitter than our own. If we had not always lived beside water, our troubles would have been greater, unbearable, insurmountable. Father would say that wherever we go, we follow our fate along waterways. It was as if the good Lord had drawn a pathway for us on Earth.

Only Father knew the secret places where we could arrive on the other shore of hope. He had long prepared for this journey through the alchemical laboratory of his books. His close friend wondered, as did we children, why Father was carrying books about eels with him as our rowboat set out from the spot where the river, there a watery arc, spilled into the lake, the same spot where the great path of the Balkan eels was said to begin.

Our trip began at night, our hope illuminated by stars. We could not have crossed the border in daylight, even though there were no border guards on either side. The border changed so quickly that guards could not arrive in time to protect it. The strong lake waves often shifted the borders, so you could no longer tell the border of one country from the other. The weather and the waves had to calm before the border could return to its old place (as long as the long coiled iron rope had not broken) or the white rubber and metal buoys, on which the gulls so often alighted, reappeared. Our old family friend was at the helm; Father rowed. Our path was not long, but it stretched on in our dreams.

As we crossed the border, the last faithful stars left us behind. The eye of the sun splashed us with its brightness. Across the smooth surface of the lake, it reflected silvery shafts of light. Father was certain we were faithfully following the path of the eels. He picked up the old spyglass he had brought long ago from Constantinople. His family had been surprised when Father returned home with a spyglass, which had taken on its own mythology in the family history. His father was the one most pleased with the spyglass. He had been condemned to live a solitary life by the shore of this lake. His close kin had all crossed the border: first his brothers and sisters, then other family members. When he saw his eldest son returned from Istanbul with a large spyglass in hand, he could not have been happier. He had thought earlier that if anyone remained abroad in Turkey, it would be this one, his eldest, and he took childlike delight in his son's return and with the spyglass. At daybreak, he would head down to the lakeshore. When the sky was most translucent, he would look at the opposite shore across the border. He walked along, peering through the spyglass. As he traveled the shore, he imagined himself the captain of a forgotten ship. Many years had passed since then. Grandfather vanished in a splendid dream with the spyglass in his hand, beside the lake. The spyglass would have been left, forgotten, had Father not taken it with him on our voyage across the lake.

After that long night of uncertainty, with fear our greatest companion, the first rays of the sun shone through. We were quite far from our native shore. We sensed we would never return.

Many years after he had purchased the spyglass in Istanbul, Father now looked through it for the first time. He pulled out all three segments; he stood at the boat's helm and began to look about. First, he aimed towards the Albanian shore, where he sought his own house, on whose doorstep he had parted with his old mother. He looked fixedly toward his house, then toward the garden. He whispered something and several droplets wet his face, but we could not tell if they were from the waves that struck the sides of the boat or if my father was weeping for the first time in his life. Then he again whispered something to himself. It was not clear what he said. Perhaps he was speaking to his mother in the distance.

At one point, he aimed the spyglass skyward. It was clearly a tear that slid across the eyepiece. Father peered through the lens of the spyglass, which seemed to hold the gaze of his long-departed father. Now the son, spyglass in hand, was moving beyond his father's field of vision. He felt as if he had broken a promise. Another tear ran down the spyglass.

Father turned the spyglass toward the first harbor of our exile. His gaze landed where the river flows from the lake, by the first bridge. He was happy that we had crossed the border and arrived at the first station along the path of the eels, the path toward America.

Our arrival in that harbor, in what had seemed the Noah's ark of our fate, was for Father like discovering an exit from a labyrinth. Though to him it was clear that in the Balkans, each exit from one labyrinth was the entry into another. Fascism was at his heels, though here it had not yet taken hold. The concept of the labyrinth echoed more strongly in Father's consciousness as he discovered a new mysterious course of waters meandering through unforeseen currents.

He had been fascinated by this thought: how do the eels manage to find escape from the Balkan labyrinth? And when he discovered the secret of the path of the eels, he believed that his escape led across the globe's waterways. He had plunged into them, taking his family with him.

What awaited Father with this first departure from the labyrinth of his native land? Was he saved or even further lost? Would he find solace by entering the new labyrinth that awaited him in this city that stands where the river rises from the lake? This city was so close to his native one, yet so distant given the uncertainties it brought for our family's new life.

Father's philosophy on exile was that, by traveling in the labyrinth, being in motion, he was closer to life's essence. He was certain that there was a God, and he sought Him in the meanderings of the great river of his exile. Mother believed that the Divine was inside her and in remaining where she was.

Chapter 5

Father rented a house in Struga, where the rapid river, the eels' waterway, flows out of the lake. On the opposite shore of the river, he opened a small law office. It was difficult to say whose lawyer he was in those tumultuous times. There was injustice on all sides. Plaintiffs one day were defendants the next. The government changed hands quickly. New soldiers were inducted. The occupation continued.

At this time, prisoners waited listlessly for the new government to free them, sensing that when the old one came back into power, they would be prisoners again. Were they to escape, however, they would risk new charges. So they calmly remained in prison.

In these cursed times, one had to look out for oneself, protect one's family, and protect others. Father preserved his sense of justice and fairness, while holding to the thought that he must continue on to America with his family, following the path of the eels.

The house we rented had two wings with a long courtyard and large balconies that jutted out from the house, from which there was a wonderful view of the lake and the river.

We children quickly became accustomed to life in this town, but from our vantage point, we could not sense Father's worries at what he knew was a crossroads of labyrinths.

We soon became friends with our nearest neighbors. Those living by the lake were of various faiths and nationalities, separated by various conquerors, but not completely divided; they maintained a mutual trust. Neighborliness persisted as the most significant Balkan institution. In this way, even our poverty and wars were more easily endured.

In little time, Mother had grown close to the family of the fisherman Kocho Hadjievski, our nearest neighbor. Vaskresya and Kocho had three daughters. We shared with them whatever we had: bread and trust. Their youngest daughter, Maria, became almost like a part of our family. We all loved her. Mother loved her like a sister.

Kocho Hadjievski had other daughters, but each had followed her own path. Maria was the only one left at home. She was beautiful, tall, steadfast, with long dark hair, blue eyes, and a cheerful expression. There were rumors that she had given her heart to a young Italian soldier, before the surrender. The soldiers departed, and Maria was to remain unwed forever.

She quickly trained to become a nurse. In the far-flung villages, her renown was greater than that of the doctors. There was not a house by the lake where her goodness had not entered, where she had not healed a wound, or given an injection painlessly. Igor Lozinski, an immigrant from far-off Russia, also learned of Maria's goodness and intellect.

He had come from distant Saint Petersburg. During the Russian Civil War he had saved himself by following the path of the eels southward from the Baltic Sea. Had he stayed, he would certainly have ended up in a remote Gulag. Instead, lucky to be alive, he had followed the path of the eels along Russian and European rivers and reached this mythical place beside the world's most beautiful lake; he was prepared to devote the rest of his life to studying the living fossils that inhabit the lake.

He threw himself into this task with fervor. He was grateful to the god of exiles that his and his wife's long migration through Europe had landed them there beside that lake, in a place that was to become his fatherland. He had been a renowned specialist in intestinal microorganisms at the Military Medical Academy in Saint Petersburg. Here, fate wanted him to continue his campaign against parasitic organisms, to save people from the ever-present malaria. He even established an anti-malaria clinic and hired Maria to work there. She learned more about medicine there than she had in school. Igor Lozinski and his wife loved her as if she were their own daughter.

One evening, Maria stayed out late with Mother — the *signora*, as she called her, because Mother knew some Italian. Maria had complete trust in Mother, even confiding in her the great love she had for the Italian soldier. Back at the Hadjievskis', old Vaskresya was waiting for her husband's return, a glass of wine on the table. He had gone off with the other fishermen to wait by the river for the running of the eels.

The night deepened, but there was still no sign of either Kocho or Maria. Vaskresya was not worried about her daughter. It was always possible she would spend the night at the signora's.

The night was nearly over when the metal knocker banged against the gate. "Now who could that be?" old Vaskresya asked herself. Maria was surely asleep by now at the signora's, and Kocho knew how to open the gate door for himself.

Vaskresya could tell by the sound of the knocker whether it was soldiers, people seeking Maria for medical help, or one of the neighbors. The strike of the metal now was gentle, muffled, and sporadic. She threw a cloak over her shoulders, picked up the lantern, and set off to the outer gate. Before opening it she quietly asked who was knocking.

"It's me, ma'am. It's Igor Lozinski!"

Up until that moment, no one had ever called Vaskresya "ma'am." To the neighbors, she was Kocho's wife or Vaskresya; to the young ones she was Grandma Vaskresya. She was hearing the address ma'am for the first time and wasn't sure it as meant for her.

She had heard about this Igor Lozinski from her daughter and from others in town. "What kind of trouble has brought him to our place at this time of night? Has something happened to Kocho? Maria is nearby, and so are the other children," thought Grandma Vaskresya.

"Good evening!' said Igor Lozinski, extending his hand.

"God grant you all the best, son. Come in!"

This was the first time Vaskresya had laid eyes on this man who had become something of a legend. He was tall, with steadfast bearing, a thick, bushy black moustache, and a broad, open face.

"What good news brings you here? Kocho is out hunting eels. He has been out with the other fisherman for days, hoping for a storm, waiting, so they can trap the eels."

"I am not looking for Kocho, but Maria. I wanted to ask her about a few urgent matters at the malaria clinic that can't wait till the morning. I got back late. I didn't get there in time to see her."

Vaskresya laid out a spoonful of cherry preserves and a glass of cold water, as was the old custom when visitors arrived.

"Maria is at our neighbors nearby, at the signora's. She sleeps over there sometimes. There aren't many like them; they're from Albania, escaped in a boat across the lake. They're now our closest neighbors. The signora's husband is a lawyer. He studied in Constantinople. See that little room over there? That light shines until the crack of dawn."

Igor Lozinski looked out the window. He could see clearly the gold lamp that illuminated the shelves of books. "An exile's destiny," he said to himself. Vaskresya could tell that their neighbor's fate had caught Igor's interest:

"My daughter Maria says that when she was dusting the books in his library, she noticed that he had a lot of notes about eels, and pictures of them, too. The lawyer reads through the night and then spends his day defending people in trouble with the government. They're nice folk. They haven't been here long, but they already have many friends."

Igor Lozinski had come on ordinary business, but he sensed that he was about to meet someone who would play an important role in his life. Exile had strengthened his intuition.

"It is rather late at night, ma'am, but I have to admit that I'm curious about your neighbors, especially their books about eels!"

"Son, we're like family. We go back and forth at any time of day or night. The gateway between our houses is always open."

Grandma Vaskresya took her lantern and led her guest to the neighbor's house. Maria appeared at the door. She was surprised to see her boss standing there. There were some instruments he needed, and she told him where they were.

Father was resting after a long night of reading. In the nighttime quiet, the sounds of their conversation reached his ears. He came to the door.

"Good Evening, neighbor!" Vaskresya said, turning to him.

"Good evening," replied Father.

"This is Igor Lozinski, from the malaria clinic. He came to the house to ask Maria about some equipment there. I told him about you and your books about the eels. I said to myself, you've got books about eels, he's got books, well, it would be good for you two to meet. You're newcomers, he and his wife are too. Well, I said to myself, why shouldn't you get to know each other."

Maria was surprised by her mother's unexpected chattiness and unsure what would happen next.

Father had heard quite a bit in town about Igor Lozinski and for a long time had wanted to meet this man who had a similar history as a refugee — one of them had fled from Italian Fascism, the other from Soviet Communism. They had parallel fates. They were destined to meet and become close. Father had even seen one of Lozinski's displays of animals that live in the lake. He'd been fascinated by the model showing the path of the eels and by the two large stuffed eels on display.

According to what Father had heard, Lozinski had a wide-ranging knowledge of the migratory movements of the lake's inhabitants, especially the eels.

With that gentle look of his that always radiated a quiet vitality, he said, "My dear Vaskresya, our house is your house, your guests are ours."

Turning to Lozinski, he then said, "You do me a great honor in coming to my house, Mr. Lozinski. Maria has spoken a great deal about you, and people always talk about the good things you are doing."

"Maria has also spoken to me about you and your family," the guest replied at once. "I have wanted to meet you for a long time. Mrs. Hadjievski brought me over when I knocked on their door, telling me it was the same as if I had knocked on yours. She pointed out to me the little room with the golden lamp. She told me about the eels, too. So we came over."

"I am glad you did, it was the right thing to do. Please, come in," said Father.

"It's late for us," noted Vaskresya, turning to leave. " I'm still waiting for Kocho to get back from the traps. They're waiting for a strong wind so they can catch the eels."

Maria spoke briefly with her boss and then went to Mother's room.

Father brought Igor Lozinski to his library, where the golden lamp was shining. He turned up the lamp.

Soon the lights went out at old man Kocho's; he still hadn't returned. He was waiting for the eels.

Father poured the guest some of the rakija Grandpa Kocho had made by blending their grapes with grapes from the market. Igor Lozinski was quite familiar with the taste. But there was different flavor to this rakija that quiet Balkan night, as these two men who had wandered the earth were brought closer by the same impossible quest to follow the path of the eels. Between them that old Balkan proverb was realized: mountain cannot meet mountain, but man can meet man.

Igor Lozinski looked with genuine amazement at Father's books. He could not believe that Father's library contained such old volumes. For him, every shelf represented some compensation for each passing century in the Balkans.

He was drawn first to Father's holy books, especially the old hand-written Korans with their blue- and rose-tinted miniatures, arranged alongside a Bible and Talmud with Kabala on the topmost shelf; then there was the array of books on metaphysics, testimonies about the Jesuits, books concerning the Janissaries. He also saw books dedicated to the former empires of the Balkans and noted in particular an entire shelf devoted to the eras of their downfall.

But he really could not believe his eyes when he saw the books and old documents about eels. Father watched him, seeming to understand his wonder — they had both been working unaware of their common project, both had been fully absorbed in seeking the same goal: to find the path of the eels. They searched for it as if seeking their own exit, but without success. Now the god of exiles had merged their fates so they could find at last the path of the eels, the path of their return from exile.

Chapter 6

The night was long and cold. But this Mediterranean lake managed to tame the winter chill. In the gardens of several houses, palms were growing, protected from the cold as if they were members of the family. Figs and lemons also matured and ripened. The almond trees blossomed early.

Igor Lozinski traveled through the eternity of Father's books. He reached the Eastern manuscripts. He immersed himself in the old records that Father hoped might reveal the lost Ottoman era. Father was searching the path of the eels for an exit from the Balkans, but also continued his search through the old Ottoman documents, which he needed to settle himself and his family firmly in the Balkans. He did not know which path we should ultimately take: the path of the manuscripts — of a lost Atlantis — or the path of the eels. At the end of each pathway the family's salvation lay hidden.

In the distance, the dark clouds had finally begun to disperse, and from time to time, a star shone through. From the nearby mountain, its whitened summits marking the border between two countries, cold wind carried a sprinkling of rain. Suddenly, loud voices and the banging of sheet metal and old pots could be heard from all sides. Fires were lit, and torches moved along the shores of the lake and river.

Even though night had passed, lights were being lit all through the neighborhood, and women and children went out, hurrying toward the lake to keep the fishermen company as they waited for the eels. Father and Igor Lozinski set aside the books. They looked out through the window at the torches illuminating the lake. Igor Lozinski was first to speak.

"The eels are heading out of the lake," he said, "leaving the Balkans; they are setting off through the rivers out to the distant seas and oceans."

As he said this, his thoughts were transported to the distant Baltic, to the cold North Sea, to the place where the eels departed from his native city. Something trembled in his exile's soul, something that stirred in Father's as well.

"The path of the eels," said Father, "the path of our cursed hope of return ... "

Loud voices approached the house. A lamp had been lit at the Hadjievskis'. With teakettle in hand, Mother entered the room. She saw Father and Igor Lozinski looking with sad eyes at the fire beside the lake. She greeted their guest before slipping back out. It had been an abundant, a very abundant, eel hunt. They watched old Kocho carry a basket of eels on his back. The cluster of burning torches added to the people's joy from this successful catch.

Eventually the commotion died down. No matter how successful the hunt had been, many eels continued on their path.

Although Father and Igor Lozinski had known each other only a short time, their life experiences had drawn them close. There was a long silence that Igor Lozinski was first to break.

"People are happy with the catch, but many eels will continue on their journey of renewal. No matter how many are captured on their journey, the eels will return, revitalized by countless new offspring," he said. Father listened attentively. He could easily penetrate the thoughts of this learned and intelligent man.

Father considered the eels' journey from the point of view of myth and metaphysics, seeking a utopian solution. With the fortitude of a self-taught man who had spent years studying the migrations of the lake's birds and fish, he constructed his own dialectic game of existence. So long as man did not destroy the migratory cycle of the birds and especially the eels, he could remain happy anywhere on this Earth.

Father wanted to describe to his new friend the results of his search through his subconscious, strengthened by his strong intuition — namely, the parallels he had drawn between the passing of Balkan empires and the migratory cycles of the birds and fish, the eels in particular. Igor Lozinski, both a biologist and medical researcher, was deeply engaged in Cartesian study of the living organisms in the lake and river; this made Father hesitant to reveal his thoughts, because he did not want Lozinski to dismiss him as an overzealous amateur. But that is not how things turned out.

There was room here for expanding their friendship, especially when Igor Lozinski saw the sort of books Father read about the migratory movements of the lake's birds and fish, especially the eels. Father was happy to have met, at last, a person in the Balkans to whom he could entrust his greatest dream, held so close to his heart: to leave by following the path of the eels. He believed that good fortune had given him this great friendship in the Balkans.

When Father first learned the story of the eel's migration path and its return through new generations, it gave him strength to persist in his battle with exile. That night, as he explained the uncertain path of his family and compared it with the path of the eels, he entrusted to Igor Lozinski his principal theory that everything occurring in nature could be affirmed in the human spirit.

He explained, still with his self-taught reasoning, that natural phenomena are clearly mirrored in the human spirit. If that mirror were broken, tremendous human suffering would ensue.

Silence fell on that night of the fruitful eel hunt and Igor Lozinski, gripped by Father's thoughts, broke the silence to speak.

"Since time immemorial, the eel has followed the eternal river, a bridge flowing between the lake and the seas. The eel accomplishes the round trip during the course of its life and the life of its descendants."

Father was delighted that Igor Lozinski had gone right to the core of the matter. He could not believe that into his house by the river there had appeared this person who had also dedicated his life to the mystic path of the eels. Even in his dreams, he could not have found a better interlocutor.

Lozinski had fled his country, and by saving himself from Stalinism, he had saved his very life; Father, in his flight across the lake, was saving himself from Fascism. These two exiles from two opposite currents along the path of the eels had found each other beside this river, flowing from the lake, through which the surviving eels were now traveling in the dark Balkan night.

For the first time they spoke openly to each other, like brothers in fate, explaining their motives for giving themselves over to the path of the eels. They explained how, through their wanderings across Europe, they had come to understand the life cycle and pathway of the eels.

As he looked out at the last remaining flames of the fishermen's torches and immersed himself in the stillness in which the town — satisfied with the eel hunt — had fallen asleep at last, Igor Lozinski quietly continued.

"Now the surviving eels are traveling happily down the river. Actually, it is the female eels that travel after their long peaceful and harmonious sojourn in the lake. They follow the river to the ocean, to the cradle of their birth, where their lives end in love. There they transfer their genes to a new generation, thus realizing the testament of that love."

Father was well aware of this hypothesis about the eels' epic journey. He listened enthralled to Igor Lozinski, who understood the secret natural phenomena of the lake, and as Father listened, his great capacity for connecting ideas was at work.

First, he imagined his family traveling along the path of the eels; he alone could find reason for such a comparison and was not sure that he should share this with his new friend. Then, he drew parallels with the imagined heroic return of the eels. After all, is not the path of the eels simply an organic, living embodiment of the cycle of life and death?

Now here was this Russian, whose remarkable fate in exile, so similar to his own, had drawn Father closer to the lake from which he wanted to move away, to follow the path of the eels.

Chapter 7

The surviving eels — at times in large clusters, at times in a single column — were driven by strong instinct, and despite every possible trap set by nature and man, they continued their eternal migration.

As the eels moved off into the distance, Father's inner restlessness to follow them grew; in their journey he hoped to find a model for his exit from the Balkans. If eels knew the pathway, why had people forgotten it? This is what Father was thinking during the stormy night of the eels' departure.

The commotion had long since died down, and the torches of the eel hunters had been extinguished. Not even the wind blew with its earlier force. Father needed complete quiet, the quiet of his opened books, to calm within him the disquiet that had grown during the course of the day. In the dark Balkan night, pulsing with the rhythmic sound of the lake's waves, Father continued to search for his Balkan Atlantis, which had once been abandoned, and with it the happy circle of life ended, but whose rediscovery now seemed possible by following the path of the eels.

As a strategy in exile Father wanted a return to his self, to his own identity even as he sought a way into a new exile. Having found no resolution to his own utopian dreams, nor any credible models among humans or in human history, he had resigned himself, in this era of Fascism and Stalinism, to seek the salvation offered by the path of the eels. He was particularly impressed by the eel's ability to adapt and transform itself in order to overcome the tremendous forces of destruction it encountered on its way. In his thoughts, he never ceased comparing his family's path with the eels' behavior and continual metamorphoses along their path.

That night, as the eels departed, Father listened to his new friend from distant Russia describe more fully the transformation of these creatures, and he could not help but think how similar fate was for all exiles.

Igor Lozinski could not have known Father's thoughts, but he sensed his agitation when he spoke of the metamorphoses of the eels along their great journey.

"At its core, the journey of the eels is tragic. While they live in the lake, they are symbols of life and endurance. But they do not remain in its calm and fresh waters. Some secret force pulls them toward the watery distances."

"Well, hadn't it been like that for our family by the lake?" thought Father as he listened with fascination to his friend. "Has nature not deceived us so that we remain here to live out our lives in these harmonious regions? Why don't we also depart on that tragic and uncertain journey?"

"The eels want to spend their lives in the lake, but they end it in the ocean!" continued Igor Lozinski.

"We also leave the lake, hoping to live happily somewhere else," Father replied.

"There are many riddles associated with the eels on their path that man has not yet been able to unravel. But the most amazing thing happens during their metamorphoses."

For a moment, Father's expression changed. It was clear that his new friend was now addressing his obsession with the metamorphoses that the eels undergo during their great journey to the ocean.

"Before it is seized by the impulse to embark on its journey, the path to renewal and death," continued Igor Lozinski, "the eel has a bright silvery color, but the moment it sets off, its back becomes a dark greenish olive color; then it turns black, but shiny, while the sides of its belly retain their bright silver. On the eve of departure, the eel's eyes grow two to three times larger."

While listening, Father's thoughts traveled to America, along the path of the eels. Departure for America was, in fact, still the intended plan for our family's exile. After we had crossed the border and become immigrants, there was a period when we could easily have continued on to America or Australia.

My mother was instinctively against travel to America. She felt an obligation to maintain the family's gravitational pull to its native land, but for Father, the family's equilibrium would be maintained only by relocating the family's center of gravity. As time passed, opportunities for the family to relocate to America strengthened Father's resolve to follow the path of the eels to its shores.

As he listened, enthralled, to Igor Lozinski, Father's thoughts turned momentarily to the trips of various family members across sea and ocean on that fateful night of division, when some chose the path of the eels' departure, and others the path of their return.

The former headed to Europe and America, the others to the Balkans and Asia. Both branches of the family had their fates transformed; they underwent all kinds of adaptation and metamorphosis — just like the eels during their long migration — Father thought as he listened, rapt with attention, to Igor Lozinski's words.

Increasingly, Father maintained a mystical belief in the path of those eels, which were guided by some divine force. And a belief that the eels — weren't they known as divine prophets, indeed, a role that was ascribed to them in distant mythologies — would show him and our family the true path toward an exit from this cursed cycle of exile. Didn't every possible danger lurk on our path, too, just as on the path of the eels? Flight remained a last chance for endurance and survival.

Igor Lozinski clearly sensed the parallel Father was drawing between the pathways of humans and the path of the eels, between migration in nature and the migration of people throughout the course of history.

As he listened, thoughts of the eel filled Father's mind and he wondered if there was a resolution to the contradictions between his inner world and the external one. He thought, "Eels die where they are born, in the place fate has given them deep in the oceans, unreachable by humans. But we humans, poor things, are born in one place, and no one knows where we are fated to die."

Father's system of associations, which had grown stronger in his exile, was constantly renewed, inspired by the juxtaposition of the fate of humans with the fate of the eels. As he listened to his learned friend describe the natural saga of the eels with such precision, he could not stop looking for new links between the movement of his family and the path of the eels.

After the heroic journey, after the ecstasy of spawning the next generation, don't the bones of the eels sink and disappear in one place? They end in the ocean depths at the very source of their birth and their death.

But what happened to the bones of our people who had set out along the path of the eels and were forgotten during their endless meanderings? Some of our descendants, caught in the path of the eels, would have been left for eternity in a foreign land, and so used their last will and remaining funds to have their bones sent back to their native land — believing that it alone could receive them and give them rest and that only there could their bones sink deep down into the soil, as the bones of eels sink down to the bottom of the sea.

As Father thought and Igor Lozinski talked, the eels continued on their path. The Balkan night deepened there at that place where the river springs from the great lake. In the distance, amidst the dark clouds, several stars appeared. The eels that had not been captured, raced, invisible, toward the sea, with their unrelenting instinct for survival.

At some point, Father and Igor Lozinski grew quiet, each with his own thoughts, and gazed toward the river flowing past.

Mother had still not slept. Once she had finished the chores she had planned to complete the next day, she quietly stole up to his study to watch him through the night, as if in this way she were taking on her share of the responsibility for the voyage that Father contemplated and which one day might become reality. She looked for some reason to enter.

She had long followed the swirling current of Father's thoughts about the eel. She secretly feared that Father might implant the idea of the eels in a second or third person, and that could lead them into unforeseen difficulties. She feared that this was happening already. She now entered the room, whether she would be seen or not. Softly, she glanced toward the half-opened window. Father and Igor Lozinski, deeply immersed in their thoughts and their conversation about the eels, did not feel the cold. Mother quietly closed the window, then stole imperceptibly from the room. As she slowly moved away, she could hear Igor Lozinski. He was still talking about the open circle as a symbol of the eel's journey.

"The eel's movements, my respected friend, symbolize a circular, temporal current. The circle has always fascinated man. It has its own rhythmic, restorative tempo between cosmic time and transcendence. The eel stands in relation to symbols of the father and the mother. The mother is connected to the symbol of the sea, the father to the land and the earth. Isn't it striking, this closeness between the mother and father and the eel? They are marked by self-sacrifice and eternal birth. No eel has seen its offspring, nor has any offspring lived to discover its mother."

Father listened to Igor Lozinski with excitement, and in his mind, the inescapable associations between eels and humans grew stronger. He quietly remarked:

"Haven't some of our people been forced to set off across the ocean in search of their livelihood without having seen their children left behind with their mothers, and then the day came when those children, too, set off along the path of the eels, following the path of their fathers?

Igor Lozinski was surprised by Father's words. He listened, setting aside his own thoughts. Father, more for his own benefit, continued:

"The eels return from the oceans through their offspring. Yes, the eels have a fatherland for their birth, and a fatherland for their death, while we are left with neither."

Here the conversation ended. Father gave Igor several books about eels with which he was unfamiliar. Dawn was breaking when they parted.

Mother had finally fallen asleep, but not for long. She dreamt of the eels swimming up the river. Those now on their path to the ocean would have passed through her native land.

Father walked about the small space of his library deep in thought. He glanced once more toward the river, where the eels had passed on their great journey. He took down another book from his library and sat in the large armchair. On the first page, he at once fell asleep, worn out by the path of the eels.

Mother woke from her light sleep, went into the study, put out the lamp, and spread a blanket over Father. She watched over the rest of her husband's sleep. She knew how precious it was to help him handle whatever events would arise in the new day.

Chapter 8

That deep, dark, and gloomy Balkan night when the eels — their ranks decimated—left the lake was strongly etched in Father's memory. How strong the instinct for survival was in the life cycle of the eels, he thought, but his mind was on the fate of our family.

The night also held significance for him because of his unexpected acquaintance with Igor Lozinski, whose reflections and theories, suffused with scientific evidence about the broader implications of the eels' migration, came at the right time, just when Father was working out the most significant decision in the family's history: whether or not to set out along the path of the eels.

That night, more than ever before, the eel seemed to him a divine herald. Its life and circular voyage along Earth's waterways captivated him still more after he had heard everything Igor Lozinski told him. When captivated by a new idea, he would always change the order of books in his library to reflect that idea, and that's what he did again this time. He set up a new place for his books about eels, pushing aside other sections with books whose ideas were outdated.

Now Aristotle's *History of Animals* held a place of honor in his library. Father was quite captivated by his study of eels. There was also an old work by Herodotus in which the eel was venerated. Herodotus considered the eel the most mysterious living creature on the planet, and he placed it at the summit of Mt. Olympus. Philosophical works of Francis Bacon relating to the path of the eels also found a place of honor on the shelves.

Father did not conceal his pleasure that the scientist Igor Lozinski would accompany him on his quest to trace the path of the eels. He was inspired by his new friend, this uprooted White Russian, for the bravery he'd displayed when fate cast him as a victim. In those dark and uncertain times when Fascism ruled in Europe, Igor Lozinski had rescued himself from Stalinism in his own country and, following the path of the eels, reached the shores of this lake, where he remained faithful to his study of parasitic microorganisms, and the lake's fish and birds, in particular their migratory routes.

It was clearer to no one more than to Father why in this time of discord, when war threatened to destroy centuries of harmony, Igor Lozinski would want to immerse himself in the study of the billions of microorganisms that had lived in harmony in the lake for hundreds of thousands of years before the arrival of humans.

Igor Lozinski, whom fate had condemned to bitter exile, abandoning Russia in flames, found safe harbor where the river flows from the lake. After the loss of his fatherland, Russia, the lake became his homeland. His exile led to happiness. Father had taken his family and left his fatherland and home by the lake following the path of the eels to seek his ultimate homeland.

When Father's path crossed Igor Lozinski's, he acquired new and convincing scientific arguments supporting his desire to continue on the circular path of exile and continue his quest to discover the secret of his family's identity. For Father, following the path of the eels also meant uncovering the circle of his family's migration, disrupted time and again by Balkan history.

And now, just when Father was at the zenith of his quest to find old Ottoman documents which held the secret of his family's identity, his quest for a lost cursive Atlantis — a manuscript containing the history of Balkan nations, people who had departed or disappeared under Ottoman rule — he changed course to discover the natural laws governing the evolution of the living creatures in the lake. This Russian whose fate had brought him such great distances intensified Father's hopes that he could set off along the path of the eels.

These were, however, cursed times in the Balkans. While the face of Fascism may have changed, its intentions had not. The Italian occupation was ending and another beginning. The Italians, like actors in some grand farce, were little prepared for real war. Many left their bones in the Balkans, others joined the Partisan resistance, still others hid themselves in mountain village homes, ready to do any type of labor to avoid discovery.

Father and Igor Lozinski were likely the last Balkan utopians prepared to follow the path of the eels across the planet's waterways, joining to it their fate. But each was motivated by his own personal motives. As for Father, he wanted to leave the Balkans with his family in heroic fashion, following the path of the eels, seeking an imagined planetary harmony most fully realized in the natural world.

Not much time passed before Igor Lozinski came to visit Father again. As before, he went first to the Hadjievskis'. Kocho was preparing some of the eels he had caught for drying, others for smoking. Never before had there been such an abundant eel catch, and it was still not over. One last big surge of eels was expected to leave the lake. The smell of the eel Vaskresija was roasting under the curved cast iron lid spread across the yard.

"Good morning, Kocho!" Igor Lozinski interrupted the old fisherman's quiet, happy tune.

"God grant you all the best, my friend!" replied Kocho.

"It's been a rich eel harvest this year!"

"It's never been better! We weren't tricked by the Maccabee Days this year. We knew exactly when the eels would set off on their long journey. We're expecting one more surge. According to our Maccabee predictions, tomorrow's going to bring a strong wind, a storm, and some fog that will get the last of the eels going."

Igor Lozinski knew about such predictions based on the days of the holy Maccabean martyrs, between the fourteenth and twenty-fifth of August. The weather predictions for the next twelve months were based on changes in the sky over the course of these summer days dedicated to the martyred Maccabee brothers.

Each quarter or eighth of a day corresponds to a calendar month. And so from generation to generation, each August, the fishermen look constantly up at the sky; they study every cloud and fix their gaze on it; they measure the temperature in the shade, and within each rainfall, they discover something of significance for the coming year.

Kocho Hadjievski was considered one of the best prognosticators of weather according to the Maccabees. His fame had spread around the lake and beyond. Other fishermen, also skilled prognosticators, came to see him both to confirm and expand their own predictions.

Father arrived while Kocho was talking about the Maccabees. He greeted Igor Lozinski. He had already seen Kocho that morning. Father also knew about the weather forecasts made according to the Maccabees, but had never looked into the subject. Now he, too, listened attentively to his neighbor. Kocho had a good idea what even the smallest cloud in the blue sky would bring. He easily predicted storms that came down from the mountain separating the two lakes. But he was especially adept and precise in sensing just the moment in the storm when the eels would leave the lake.

Old Kocho had no inkling of what other night battles his neighbor and Igor Lozinski, now glancing toward the sky and the river, were waging with the eels. And had Kocho known about the path they sought, he would surely have looked at them with surprise and pity that they were squandering their time on an unattainable desire.

It was quite a day for eels. Old Vaskresija lifted the lid on the pan in which she had set the roasted eel, now freed of its layer of fat and laced with garlic and spices. Its smell mixed with those of other eels baking in the neighborhood.

It was lunchtime and Kocho invited everyone for roast eel. Vaskresija also brought out a jug of wine. The old fisherman was in high spirits and began to sing quietly. In the distance, gunshots could be heard; the end of the war was nearing. When lunch ended, Father and Lozinski went through the side gate linking the two houses and entered Father's library while the old fisherman poured out a little more wine and finished the fisherman's song he had begun.

Chapter 9

"Anonymous waters know all our family's secrets," Father confided in Igor Lozinski as they entered the library. He told him about his family's devotion to life at the water's edge: by the sea, the lake, or the rivers. "Along our family's path of exile, water has shown us a possible way out."

Along those waterways, Father was not seeking infinitude, but depth. It was not without reason that Father told Igor Lozinski that deep waters flow slowly, shallow ones quickly. Water set the rhythm of our family's exile.

"The lake is unusually calm. The storm Kocho predicted is brewing," Father said, closing the windows that Mother had opened wide, hoping it would air out the books.

Father and Igor Lozinski, with the inner strength of two men suffering in exile, both sensed the metamorphoses taking place in the space between water and sky, between people and the lake's rich flora and fauna. This land around the lake was like a paradise, and it seemed to touch the very origin of life, both its continuity, and its transience. There was here an enduring regenerative, eternal substance; here Father and Igor Lozinski had discovered a shared fatherland: a fatherland just within their grasp, yet always fleeting.

Gazing at the water, Father was struck as always by the suggestive force of its current, that perpetual flow in which lives changed, departed, remained anonymous myths for eternity. He looked at the setting sun as it spilled its last rays onto the earth, turning the blueness of the water into slowly darkening shades.

When Father sensed that he was reaching the heavens, he would usually slip lightly into sleep, but then snap awake, back into reality, searching the rapid current of the waters for the lost steps of time past. His migratory blood would draw him away from the lake in the coming spring, away from the season when the intoxicating aroma of the blossoming almonds and the bluish-golden wallflower spreads. Surely, he would carry them in his soul, and as though in an herbarium, he would turn to the memories of the lake from his past life where he had left his mother in the doorway of his native home, to the graves of his ancestors, to the origins of his lasting melancholia in exile. This would give him comfort as he followed the path of the eels. And now, before the fateful turning of this important page in his life, fate had brought him close to the Russian Igor Lozinski.

Father had returned to the Balkans after the fall of the Ottoman Empire, when his inability to follow his mother's lineage had condemned him to a new search. The fate of his Russian friend seemed to him both intimate and instructive. He, too, had left an empire, the Russian Empire, during its collapse, when another empire threatened, that of Stalinism.

Given the choice of serving Stalinism or risking the mortal danger of escape, Igor Lozinski had chosen exile. He had set out from the opposite end of the eels' route and reached the destination that Father was leaving behind. Father and Igor Lozinski had much to tell each other during those divisive and uncertain times.

The storm drew closer. The dark clouds from the nearby mountain were suspended above the spot where the river left the lake. The season's storm paralleled the storm of events. One could glimpse the end of Fascism, during whose reign Father wished to set off some restless night, along the path of the eels. He was fortunate to have finally found in the Balkans this singular person to whom he could tell the whole truth, someone who could understand him possibly better than anyone else, someone who could give him the courage to persevere with his chimerical ideas.

First, however, Father wanted to acquaint Igor Lozinski with his life project, the writing of the *History of the Balkans through the Collapse of Its Empires*. Obsessed with the changeable history of the Balkans, where compelled by fate, nations always had to begin anew, he sought something constant in natural phenomena, and in the discovery of a possible escape from there. In discovering the path of the eels, Father firmly believed that he had also discovered a path for humanity toward a true harmony with nature. This infused him with the courage to research with more determination the major migratory movements of the peoples of the Mediterranean, along with the migration of birds and fish, as part of his great project.

Over the course of three millennia, the Mediterranean never ceased attracting peoples in their exodus from the steppes, deserts, and primeval forests. And those peoples, who had themselves barely set down roots on the shores of the Mediterranean — these Greeks, Arabs, Turks — then attempted to impose their dominion over the others.

"Each empire in the Balkans, from the Roman to the Ottoman," Father confided to Igor Lozinski, "had its own long-standing rhythm of ruling. Later, they were less violent than even the weakest modern state."

At first, Igor Lozinski, who had assumed they would continue their conversation about eels, could not understand where Father was going with this discussion of Balkan empires. But Father had no intention of moving far from the topic of the eels.

"The great empires of the Balkans," he said, "but also more broadly of the Mediterranean, had a different concept of borders. Don't forget, my dear friend, that people lived for five centuries in the Ottoman Empire without borders. They were close to one another, and turning to one another, they were immersed in different languages, cultures, ways of cooking, and customs. But in the modern era, states are founded precisely on the basis of borders."

"Don't forget borders that have been imposed by ideologues," added Igor Lozinski, thinking of changes in Russia after the October Revolution.

"Of course, you're right," Father agreed. "Here, too, Fascism has set new borders and new divisions."

"But why did the collapse of those empires lead to the greatest movement of people and the creation of new borders?" asked Igor Lozinski, encouraging Father to continue.

"This question occupies a central place in my research and my ideas about experiences following the fall of the Ottoman Empire. The Balkan nations have been emerging with difficulty from the tunnel of the Ottoman period for about the last century and a half, and will likely continue with difficulty. After the fall of the Ottoman Empire, there was no end to the massive expulsions and resettlement of peoples of different faiths and ethnicities. This century has flowed past, but divisions and relocations have not ended. You are correct, my dear friend, that ideology will divide people even more, and it will seek justification for its past expansion at the cost of new horrors."

Although in one way, Father and Igor Lozinski were digressing from the topic of the eels, in another, they were drawing closer to it.

"Well, my friend," Igor Lozinski responded, "when I hear you speak about people and borders, my thoughts turn to eels and borders."

"What is the connection you're making?" my father said after a moment.

"I see it clearly; I can sense it," said Igor Lozinski. "The end of Fascism is evident. That empire of evil founded on racial intolerance and discrimination is, fortunately, at its end. Millions of innocent people have perished, and will perish. Fascism will be defeated, that is certain, but there are new concerns."

Igor Lozinski stopped talking. The night storm resounded in thunderclaps and rain. Where the river left the lake, fishermen's torches were lit again. A hush fell, broken from time to time only by the fishermen's shouts meant to frighten the eels. Then came the familiar sounds of banging on sheet metal, the reedy wail of zurlas, the beat of drums.

"These are lucky times for the eels," Igor Lozinski said, turning to a new theme, but with his previous thought still in mind.

Father looked at him quizzically.

"How can these be lucky times when so many of the eels are dying?"

"Others will save themselves and continue on the path. The eels' pathway is still there."

Father was not sure exactly where Igor Lozinski was heading, even when he added:

"The eel, my friend, is a true symbol of sacrifice. If God exists, he is also surely embedded in the eels' power to regenerate after being severed. What other living creature has such power? Even if a single eel manages to slither past the merciless fishermen, that is enough for the path to continue and for the renewal of a new generation. Such is the path of the eels; it is both heroic and tragic."

Father was pleased that the conversation was shifting back to the eels, and although he was still not completely sure exactly where his friend's words were heading, he could sense what it might be.

"May this country never experience a time when a tyrant dares to cut off the path of the eels," continued Igor Lozinski.

"There could be no greater sin than that!" said Father.

"An even greater misfortune would be if an exit to the Mediterranean, the Atlantic, and the world, were blocked," added Igor Lozinski. "If the country is condemned to permanent isolation, then the path of the eels would stop."

"How would someone dare to cut off this holy path of the eels?" asked Father.

"It is possible. Anything is possible!" replied his friend, but he had still did not reveal to Father his great secret about how the pathway of the eels had been severed in his former fatherland, Russia. At times, Father came close to uncovering Igor Lozinski's secret. He nearly chanced on it, and his curiosity grew. But he was patient. There was still a great deal for them to tell each other, many books and notes about the eels to be exchanged.

In the distance, the torchlights were flickering. The calls of the fishermen slowly died away. Many eels had managed to save themselves while others waited for another night to depart. Igor Lozinski was first to break the silence:

"What mysterious command gets transmitted to the eels? What common signal sends them all on their great voyage across the ocean, leading them from the fresh waters of the continent toward their common spawning grounds in the deep heart of the Atlantic?"

Father was considering how to answer this question when Igor Lozinski continued.

"There is a single signal for all the eels on the planet that happens simultaneously. The same power compels them toward their last encounter with life and death — a powerful and wonderful harmony that people will surely never attain. The movement of this swarm of eels connects the seas, the oceans, the continents."

Father listened with delight. He, too, was engrossed in the study of migrations and of the fish living in the lake, but he was an autodidact and so was pleased for the opportunity to hear for the first time how scholars understood the path of the eels. This narrative transported him to an indelible picture, to a recollection from his life by the lake: Sometimes while at the shore, he would look up at the sky. His glance would fix momentarily on a flock of birds in flight. Preoccupied with the mythic path of the eels in the waters, this flight of birds always excited him. Everything was eternally in flight in this pure crystalline oasis, our planet Earth. And the messages coming to him from the waters and from the heavens were always the same: depart … depart.

Father discovered prototypes of human migration in the migratory movements of fish and birds. Their cyclical movements were incited most by the search for new places, better conditions for continuing their lives. These natural phenomena interested him because he could compare them with human lives, especially the life of his own family. He was fascinated by the lake birds that after a long flight across the world would, at certain seasons, return to die in the nests in which they had been born. He also watched birds that flew erratically past their native nest, because, he thought, they most likely had lost some internal mechanism, and now headed mindlessly toward their death. This unusual act brought Father's thoughts to an impasse, and he sought a new direction. As he sought resolution to his own destiny, he was fascinated by this correlation between the animal world and the human.

His thoughts were occupied, more than ever before, with the question of how people — like birds and eels — could be gripped by the same instinct to return to the starting point of their existence as the end of life approached. In his musings, Father continued to seek similarities in the conditions that compelled the greatest migrations of people and the conditions under which the migrations of birds, fish, and other animals unfolded.

In his historical research of the fall of the Balkan empires, at a time when he was also studying animal migrations, he — led by his innate gift to make quick comparisons — sought similarities between these migrations and the invasions of the hordes of Genghis Khan and Tamerlane. Hunger propelled them, but so too did a drive for movement and displacement regardless of the sacrifice in order to migrate to new lands.

Contemplating his own complex identity, he imagined that he possessed some distant gene from those who were part of these great migrations. While studying the fate of Arctic lemmings, he asserted that they never desire to return to their native land but die in the lands of their exile. Somewhat, perhaps, like Genghis Khan and his descendants.

Igor Lozinski inquisitively followed the course of Father's thought while continuing his own.

"There exists no force that can change the direction of the eels' movement. There is no force ... but, I hope to God it is never found."

He cut short this thought, but it mingled with another unmentionable one, which he still did not want to share with Father. After composing himself a moment, Igor Lozinski continued.

"The power of the eels to maintain unerring direction in their migration has been compared by scientists to the orientation of birds — migratory birds. However, two different phenomena are at work here. Some French scientists who have long studied the path of the eels attribute this phenomenon, their perfect sense of direction, to a sort of atavism."

"What sort of atavism?" Father asked.

"According to these French scientists, the European eel, during its travels in the distant past, populated the lost Atlantis, which was located near its spawning grounds. But when Atlantis disappeared forever into the ocean depths, the eels, by instinct and atavism, returned to the same place in order to continue the process of regeneration."

"Instinct and atavism?" repeated Father in a whisper. For him the lost Atlantis was in fact a lost fatherland. He did not believe in return from exile, in a return to the lost paradise of his childhood, to his native home. Listening to how the eels had confronted their migration at a time when Atlantis existed on Earth, and then how they discovered their elusive path following the great fracture of our planet, he attempted to follow the current of associations in his mind, a mind strengthened in exile, to find a path to his own lost fatherland by following the path of the eels.

Science has borders, then, that myth erases, Father thought, while listening with fascination to Igor Lozinski. But the Russian continued along a circuitous path, avoiding what he feared the most: that someone in the Balkans would cut off forever the eternal path of the eels.

It was late at night. The town had long since fallen asleep. Mother could no longer be heard in the kitchen. Father listened eagerly to Igor Lozinski's story, waiting for him to lay out his fears about the interruption of the path of the eels, which, in his view, must happen eventually.

They parted in early morning. As Igor Lozinski left, he invited Father to come see his collection of lake flora and fauna. Their shared interest in the eels, as well as their similar human fates, had brought them to something much closer than a usual friendship.

Father stayed awake a bit longer after Igor Lozinski left to page through the books about eels that his friend had brought him. A light sleep overtook him. The weather stirred. A storm was brewing.

"The last eels must surely now be on their merry way," said Father, half-asleep.

The rest of his sleep was tormented by thoughts of the force that could disrupt the path of the eels.

Chapter 10

It was a glorious sunny day. Sunshine radiated on all sides. The sun's rays appeared to penetrate deep down in the waters, lighting it with every shade of blue.

Father, followed by Mother's faithful gaze, set out along the river. He reached the spot where the river flows from the lake. The waters tumbled loudly. He came to this spot before making important decisions in his life. He confided in the waters. He spoke with them, gazing toward the opposite shore of the lake, the shore of his exile. He spoke with his mother. He believed the waves carried to the threshold of their home, set on a small piece of land along the famed Via Aegnatia, the truth about his possible exit toward Atlantis. In the flow of the waters he felt the rhythm of transience, to which he quietly abandoned himself. He had made his firm decision to depart along the current of these waters, to follow the path of the eels.

Crossing the drawbridge, he found himself on the other bank. Here, beside the river, was his small legal office. He alone knew whom to protect and how to protect them in these difficult and uncertain times when power changed hands quickly. His law profession had placed him at a safe distance from the regime, which helped him gain the confidence of ordinary people more easily. People came to him as their last hope before facing the law. Christians and Muslims, rich and poor, came to be defended from something or someone, feeling they were not at fault, but rather victims of these misguided times. Father wondered who should be defended first in these difficult times: himself, his family, or others? The eels that had entered deeply into his consciousness, now also turned his attention from his work.

He stayed a short time in the office. He exchanged a word or two with the people who had been waiting for him since early morning. To each he gave a comforting word, advice, a message. In the middle of the table in his office sat an old typewriter he had dragged from Constantinople and on which he had often changed the letter keys according to the alphabet of the new occupiers. Some keys stood straight up; those letters he corrected in the text by hand. He typed something on the machine and then advised his young assistant what needed to be done that day, and then left.

As he set back out along the river, he had decided to visit Igor Lozinski at his home laboratory, near the antimalaria clinic. He had not left word either at home or the office where he was going, something he rarely did. When he was delayed too long, Mother usually sent one of the children to the office to see why Father was late. Perhaps he had thought to buy this or that on his way home. He understood his wife's message quite well and therefore almost never deviated from the unspoken rule that he should tell her where he was going and when he would return. But this day, carried away by the beautiful weather, the sparkle of the sun on the blue waters along the river, he set off toward his friend Igor Lozinski. He walked along, deep in thought, his worries carried away with the water.

He stopped near the first weir close to where the river flows from the lake. This barrier on the river channeling the eels through narrow passageways was thousands of years old and had always seemed to him a real labyrinth. He thought how cursed was the fate of those eels that were caught, ending their lives in this primitive labyrinth, this trap, this Balkan guillotine.

The eels had been preparing nearly a decade for their great heroic journey toward renewal across the ocean, only to be stopped by this cursed weir. Over time, the appearance of the weir had changed. The river had been dammed in the middle, and its strong current had flooded nearby fields. A cement weir had been erected. It had been raised before the eels like a veritable Balkan wall.

But a small number of the eels passed through the weir and continued on their path. Some traveled over dry land for a kilometer to pick up their path once again, joining the lucky ones that had escaped the weir.

Was Igor Lozinski thinking that these weirs could one day halt the eel migration? If they were perfected enough to block the river completely would they block the path of the eels?

Father crossed the weir, and once again, the peaceful river flowing with blue-silvery waters came into view. He had not even noticed that he had reached the home of Igor Lozinski.

His host greeted him joyfully at the gate before leading him into the house. They immediately went to the laboratory workroom, where Igor Lozinski was creating his unique museum collection of the most significant representatives of lake flora and fauna, from invisible microorganisms up to stuffed and mounted examples of the birds, fish, and mammals that lived in the lake and its environs.

Igor Lozinski introduced Father to his assistants. They were people of both Christian and Muslim faiths, and of various nationalities. Among them were renowned fishermen and hunters: the best authorities on nearly every corner of the lake region. Their know-how, talent, and great love for the lake lands combined well with the mind and knowledge of Igor Lozinski. All of them were engrossed in their teacher's great project: to create this singular collection of lake relics, of its living fossils, that appeared sentenced to disappear someday from the lake. No former empire nor any of the various regimes that had ruled the lake had managed to achieve what Igor Lozinski and his coworkers were achieving: a demonstration of the world's timeless continuity. When he came to this town to devote himself and his work to the lake region, he was motivated by the thought that continuity, in each form it takes, is the most beautiful thing in the living world.

In this region, people had lived with a constant sense of broken continuity. Lozinski set himself the task of establishing, through his collection, the continuity of life in the lake, showing the dominant forms of its flora and fauna, subject as they were to evolution and extinction. He wanted to demonstrate the continuity of this lake, over the past hundred, thousand, million years.

In those fateful years of worrying over the survival of his family in the Balkans, Father had been obsessed with the idea of continuity, not of the lake flora and fauna, but of the rule of empires. When he became acquainted with Igor Lozinski and his project, however, he began to see a broader concept of continuity and the commonality of natural and social phenomena.

Father was inspired by this man who, during a time of war and uncertainty, following his long journey from home, had devoted himself so intently to the creatures living in the lake that others did not even consider alive. Here were representatives of an entire microcosm of animals, gathered or caught in the lake, the marsh, the surrounding fields and mountains. For the first time in his life, Father saw the three types of sponges that lived in the lake — true, living relics — and also many types of arthropods that had lived an eternity in this region. There were mounted examples of the first vertebrates to take possession of the earth. There, too, were birds, fish, mammals.

Soon, Igor Lozinski's principal assistant arrived, a young biologist named Cvetan Gorski. He was actively involved in Igor Lozinski's project and had begun to love his teacher like a spiritual father. He was a hard worker, courageous, with a sharp mind. He was also Igor Lozinski's right-hand man and Igor Lozinski saw in him a likely successor. He taught Cvetan Gorski everything he knew so that he could carry on his mission, broaden it, and pass it on to new generations.

Since early childhood, Cvetan Gorski had been tied to the living world of the lake. He had learned many of its secrets and had now become its researcher. After being introduced to Father, Cvetan Gorski said, "Professor spoke to me about you. He showed me your books and notes about the eels. You have come to know many of his secrets. We are lucky that you have come to visit us and to join forces with us."

Igor Lozinski nodded.

Father could not believe the wondrous world he saw before him. Here, in one person's home, a person who had recently arrived from remote Russian realms, were gathered examples of all the ancient living creatures.

Cvetan Gorski showed Father a part of the collection devoted to several lake eels, caught just where the river leaves the lake. The eels were artfully displayed in various life phases. A large model portrayed the lake, the river, one of the weirs, and a globe with small labels marking the path of eels from the lake to the ocean and back. Looking at the model and the markings on the globe, at the true path of the eels, Father was enchanted and excited.

Here was the path that he dreamed his family would take. Cvetan Gorski noted Father's excitement.

"Professor Igor Lozinski is one of the world's leading authorities on the migratory route of the eels," he said quietly. "As a matter of fact, he proposed a route with great precision and accuracy and discovered the eels' pathway from European rivers and lakes to the Atlantic Ocean and back."

While he listened, Father's thoughts caught up with — and then moved beyond — the eels affixed to marks on the globe. Igor Lozinski's voice calling him to see the rest of the collection pulled him from this reverie.

Father traveled through the labyrinth of this unique Balkan laboratory, which had preserved the memory of an entire millennium of life in the lake. Igor Lozinski had nearly completed his collection and planned to give it to the city as a permanent exhibit. He felt that only Cvetan Gorski, his student and successor, was worthy of continuing his work. Sensing that he was nearing the end of his life, he had entrusted his collection to him. He entrusted him to guard, in the evil times that were approaching, this great wealth, the one thing he had created in his life, this collection of a thousand examples of flora and fauna, a true picture of the lake.

And now fate had brought Father, not as a lawyer to witness his last will, but as a great lover of the lake. Over a glass of rakija and a plate of meze brought by the cheerful Natasha Lozinska to the terrace looking out on the river, Igor Lozinski, Father, and Cvetan Gorski, a triple alliance, continued their conversation about the future of the museum collection and, in particular, the path of the eels.

Father wanted to find out once and for all the secret concerning the path of the eels, the secret about which Igor Lozinski had provided only a few passing hints. But the Russian was talking about his conjectures for the future, the future government, and the possibility that Stalinism would spread to countries in their region as well. This was all he spoke of and for the rest of the conversation he avoided discussing the eels with Father and Cvetan Gorski. Still, it was clear he would eventually share his secret with these two people, whose fates had become so close to his own. Father looked at his watch and saw how much time he had passed. He said goodbye to his hosts, and on leaving, he invited them to visit him soon.

Father set off along the river, to its source, toward the lake expanse. Although winter was on the doorstep, the sun still shone. He watched as it slowly sank on the horizon. The sky turned to bands of red, and the blueness of the waters darkened. Looking toward the sunset and the waters that rushed beyond him, Father was overcome by feelings of melancholy and quiet longing. He hastened his steps toward his family, who were surely worried by his long and unexpected absence.

Chapter 11

The end of Fascism was coming. The Allies and the Americans advanced, liberating the occupied European countries. From the east, the Red Army also advanced. One sensed the arrival of a new regime in the Balkans.

Father believed that, despite the great resistance put forth by the enslaved nations, after the brief empire of Fascism a new empire would likely rule. According to Father's conjectures on the course of empires, it was impossible for much time to pass before the Balkans would again be under a new empire. Following the fall and defeat of Fascism, Father was certain that Stalin, together with the Red Army and his totalitarian ideology, would use this historic opportunity to seize as much of Europe and the Balkans as he could.

Lost in thought, walking along the river, he had nearly reached home; the sun had already sunk into the lake. The light of the first stars arrived. He quickened his steps. As thoughts of empires — with Stalin the latest to reach the Balkans — marched away, his thoughts turned to Igor Lozinski and his secret about the future of the path of the eels in this town where the river flowed from the lake.

Who, in fact, was this Russian immigrant who had entered his life with such force? Was it their similar immigrant fates and their shared devotion to the lake and the path of the eels that had brought them close? Here before them was the lake that would unite them, bring them together in a strong bond of friendship.

Igor Lozinski's White Guard fate had carried him here to this lake after long wanderings across Russia, through Odessa, and on to Constantinople during the 1920s, a time when Father was also studying in that city. Father could well recall the rivers of people, Russian immigrants who, having saved themselves, were then arriving in Constantinople. He recalled this human protoplasm, the core of a nation that would find salvation around Constantinople and the islands of the Mediterranean as they gave themselves over to their destinies in exile.

They were young, energetic people between the ages of twenty and forty,

Father recalled. At that time, he had even read somewhere that Lenin had issued a decree by which Russia was to liberate itself from one hundred and fifty of its greatest minds together with their families.

As Father approached the source of the river he recalled something that Igor Lozinski once said: the Russian emigration was a new phenomenon in the history of mankind and could only be compared with the exodus of the Jews. Father found courage to endure his life in exile when he listened to Igor Lozinski speak about his own path to the lake.

Rivers of people had sought safe haven in the cities of Europe. They stopped where they were accepted, either from pity or Orthodox solidarity. Those who saved themselves often worked at low-level professions while living in their glorious past. In fact, they lived two worlds in one soul.

Father recalled, too, the words of Igor Lozinski that felt as if they had been said about his own life: "We suffered a great deal; perhaps this suffering is in one sense a weakness, but in another, higher sense, it is courage. Those who have suffered greatly, truly suffered, are rarely aggressive, their souls emit goodness and tolerance!"

These words were close to Father, as were these: "Our suffering, my dear friend, is like blindness. Our native land, the light of our eyes, has been taken from us. We have lost our outer vision, but our inner one has been strengthened. With our inner vision we see the unseen native soil, our holy native land."

When Igor Lozinski spoke like this, a powerful network of associations formed in Father's mind: on their long journey, as they move away from the lake into the seas, to the ocean depths, didn't the eels lose their outer vision and look with some inner vision toward their goal, toward the sea and their native ocean, and then, on their return, toward the lake of their ancestors?

"One needs to be denied one's native land," Igor Lozinski told my father on a different occasion, "in order to love that land with an unearthly love. Our everlasting unearthly love is what makes us, my friend, endlessly resilient, victors even in our defeat!"

The waves of fate had carried Igor Lozinski to the shores of the Bosporus with other drowning members of the White Guard who had saved themselves from their fatherland. Then both he, a graduate of St. Petersburg University in medicine and microbiology, and Father, a law graduate of the

University of Constantinople, had been led by fate to the Balkans, to the shores of this lake that offered them a homeland when they had lost all hope of returning to their native lands.

Both were condemned to a land without return. While fate may have crossed their paths in Constantinople, it brought them together again by chance here by the lake. The two of them were now drawn together, and their friendship broadened through mutual devotion to the eels and their circular path around the planet. And as the end of one era, the end of Fascism, loomed, Father and Igor Lozinski worried about the events that approached. It would surely be a turning point, and many destinies would change.

While Father was studying law in Constantinople, he had a clear understanding of Leninist–Stalinist socialism. At that time, he had also witnessed close up the policies of Ataturk, who at one point, wanted to draw closer to Stalin and the Soviet Union. He had watched the development of socialism in Western European democracies as well. Unlike Igor Lozinski, he had not, however, learned social communism from the inside. Father knew that there were many secrets he could learn from his Russian friend, secrets of both past and future times.

Pensively, Father entered the house. Here other worries, real and tangible, awaited him. Mother had sensed his approach from a distance by his footsteps. The whole house relaxed when Father entered.

Chapter 12

Mother was visibly concerned by Father's unexpected absence from work and from home. But she was not in the habit of asking him where he had been, least of all when the children were also in the house. It was hardest for her when she was alone. Alone with her uncertainty.

Mother was worried that the eels were increasingly drawing Father's attention away from family concerns and the work of the law office. She knew — she was fully convinced — that Father was becoming engrossed in developing a plan toward some unknown goal and she knew, too, that it was out of his concern for his family in these topsy-turvy times. It was his job to make such consequential decisions, and Mother, knowing the objective, would bear the consequences of the plan she sensed but scarcely understood. She needed time. In the end, she was convinced that following Father's plans would lead to things working out for the best.

When Father was deeply worried, he would slip unnoticed into his library. He calmed himself beside his books. First he would light the golden lamp. It illuminated the books, animated them. The lamp was like a warm, bright sun in our home. Here in its midst, in the library, in the quietness, the family's uncertain path in the world became determined. The books were like wings preparing the house to be ready at any moment to take flight skyward.

Father said that quietness was the voice of the books. In the quiet of the opened books, his thoughts fermented. His thought was to leave, nothing else, just leave. Through the ages there will always be migrations, he thought, just as there will always be births. But the rivers of emigrants will continue to flow, flow like the waters of the world.

It was almost midnight. But the golden lamp in Father's library continued to burn. Mother would not close her eyes until the children had eaten dinner and gone to bed. After his long absence and late return, Father had not been talkative with Mother. Mother could settle down and join the children in sleep only when Father's disquiet had settled within her. Such was their love. They were always filled with the other. Their love, in essence, calmed each the other.

Sometime around midnight, Mother knocked on the door of the library, carrying a tray with dinner for Father. It was rare that he did not eat dinner with the family. But today, he had completely forgotten about their shared meal.

After knocking, she heard Father's quiet voice. He is not sleeping, she said to herself and opened the door. He was engrossed in the pages of a book, a book about eels, of course. The golden lamp illuminated one of the book's many eels. Transfixed, held fast on the paper, but mobile, fleeting, and fast in Father's thoughts.

Father stood up, took the tray, and turned his gentle gaze to Mother. She calmed immediately; all her worry disappeared. She sat beside him while he began his dinner. He ate less from hunger, and more to calm Mother.

From time to time, the quiet was broken by the coughing of one of the sleeping children. Mother had not come at midnight to tell Father about household worries or worries about the children; it was the thought of departure that worried her. If she could only know ahead of time, she could prepare the family.

She was also surprised by Igor Lozinski's frequent visits and Father's absence from his law office. No news had come from their relatives across the nearby border. She had worries galore. She was worried in particular by Father's obsession with the eels and his friendship with the Russian immigrant. It was a period of occupations. One force had not yet put down roots before the next arrived. There were battles coming close to the lake. But as for him, it was all about the eels, nothing but the eels.

Nothing good would come of this, she wanted to say, but her complete trust in her husband calmed her, and she said nothing. Father understood her concerns; he knew the questions she wanted to ask him. He drew near her and put his hand on her shoulder. She nestled against him. They stayed like that a long time in silence. In the distance you could hear the breathing of the river, the cry of a night bird, the breathing of the children as they slept. Father felt refreshed by the energy released by the children's collective dreams.

He was first to whisper in the night.

"My dear," he said, "books have their fates. And books determine fates. I set out along this path, leading all of you with me. God alone knows whether it will all work out for the best."

Mother said nothing. She looked at the open books; she followed Father's thoughts. Here one could sense how the books seemed to come alive from all of the paging through them. They augmented our family's life. They ennobled Father's loneliness during his nights of exile. They became our first friends.

The books also offered him many possibilities and avenues for discovering others and gaining their trust and friendship. After all, wasn't it the books about eels that had brought him and Igor Lozinski together and made them friends?

There were wide margins of silence surrounding Father's long spans of reading. These books marked the borders of our family's happiness. The opening of a new book, Father said, opened a door to an unfamiliar house.

His voice rose again: "Fate brought Igor Lozinski to the doors of a house in which there were books open about eels. Believe me, my dear, it was fate alone that brought Igor Lozinski to our house. This man has a great, open, anguished soul that spreads goodness wherever it goes. He has saved thousands of people from sure death. He discovered a medicine to cure the cursed malaria that has destroyed many lives around the lake. Good fortune has sent him to us to rescue people as well as the lake with its countless animals. Yes, he is saving the lake, even from humans!"

For a long time Mother, did not respond to Father, but now she asked, "How will he save the lake from humans?"

"I am trying to discover that myself. Igor Lozinski has the key to the salvation of the lake. And that salvation is tied to fate and the pathway of the eels."

"I don't understand," Mother responded.

"At present, I don't either. There are many secrets in the life and thoughts of Igor Lozinski. He has stated clearly that if the path of the eels through the river and out to the sea and the ocean is preserved, the lake will also be saved. The people will live happily when the war ends and freedom comes."

Mother looked in bewilderment at her husband for a while longer, but she was unable to find the thread of logic that connected Father's thoughts.

But then, if the path of the eels were severed, surely that would mean a time of new uncertainties by the lake. Mother wanted to understand why the survival of the path of the eels was so important to Father: was it because they followed a path to America or was it about our return across the border back to our native home by the lake? Father could not clarify it himself. He did not know what the new era would bring. What would happen? Would Stalinism reach the lake? And if so, what would happen to the people, eels, waters, time? He believed that Igor Lozinski had a clear answer to all these questions.

In the east, the rose-colored light of the sun could be seen. The light of the day conquered the golden light of Father's lamp, while sleep had already conquered Father and Mother. Surely their dreams were joined in this moment, and together they followed the path of the eels on their long journey before the new day arrived with its new uncertainties. In the early morning hours, Mother left Father's library, certain that she was taking something significant from Father's dream.

Chapter 13

Father waited impatiently for Igor Lozinski and Cvetan Gorski's promised visit. At their meeting, Igor Lozinski was likely to divulge at last the long anticipated secret concerning the path of the eels and their fate in the era one could sense approaching.

During this time, Father was also pressed by an entirely different set of everyday, concrete problems connected with the fate of the family. He had to secure our daily bread, our family's tranquility.

These were difficult, uncertain times, times awaiting resolution. One could sense the end of Fascism. In these stormy times it was, Father would say, most important to keep your head on your shoulders. Don't raise it so high that it falls, nor hold it so low that you lose your sense of direction.

He was content with his general outlook; he could sense the direction of history. Every move had to be carefully chosen, clearly planned, so that he would not to be caught standing in history's path, allowing it with one small blow to overpower him, knock him off course, steal his hope.

He recalled the pledge of his brother who had remained in their native land with his belief that, because he had done nothing wrong to anyone, he had no reason to be afraid. Their different strategies were apparent when they parted: Father also had done no harm to anyone, but he had fled, seeking escape from those who might harm him.

In these moments, he also thought of Igor Lozinski's flight. He, like thousands of his compatriots, had not harmed anyone; he hoped to save himself from death by fleeing. In this way, Father always sought new arguments to justify the next departure. Even those poor eels, the small number that saved themselves, in their flight chose the fate of the others.

He spent days amidst his books preparing for his meeting with Igor Lozinski and his colleague. He prepared as if for some kind of holiday, a holiday of books, whose significance he alone understood.

For Father, each true book, page, line, or word hid a great truth, and through them wriggled those eels that saved themselves. Life demonstrated that each book had its own unfinished destiny. Each turn of the true page, read according to the changing order of Father's books, meant the turning of fate along the great path of the eels. Reading brought the book itself to life. Fate might turn at a comma, stop at a period, inquire at a question mark, or wonder at an exclamation point. Perhaps it was there in the incomplete sentence, the incomplete word amidst the alphabetical galaxy. Mother, always faithful to Father's books and his enigmatic reading, believed that souls were hidden within them.

A battle was waging among Father's books. Darwin's books on evolution stood in opposition to the truths contained in the holy books. And all of these stood in opposition to books devoted to new ideologies. One could almost feel the physical weight of the books in these times and in the life of our family.

Now Father's great, moveable library at the confluence of the waters — waters connecting river, lake, sea, and ocean along a single path, the most beautiful waterway on the planet, the path of the eels — held significant meaning for the family for its survival and its continuation. These books held a continuing source of memory, while the imagined migration of the eels and their return held the secret of a possible end to our family's exile by opening an actual path back to our land of no return.

During the days, as he awaited Igor Lozinski's visit, Father was more engrossed in his books and manuscripts than ever before. He rarely left his library, neglecting his work at the law office. His assistant would come with stacks of papers to receive Father's instructions. Father would quickly separate out the most important items that could be used to settle claims of clients in jeopardy; others he left for another time. Seeing Father so absorbed in his books about eels, his assistant would stand transfixed, unable to understand Father's fascination with them.

News came from Igor Lozinski that he would arrive that evening with Cvetan Gorski. A quiet excitement came over Mother. For nearly the whole day, she got the house ready and prepared dinner for the anticipated guests.

Igor Lozinski presented Mother with a beautiful bouquet of flowers, perhaps the first she had received since we had crossed the border. In those years of unrest, who would think to bring the signora a bouquet of flowers, Mother wondered.

The bouquet awoke a host of memories from her childhood in Salonika, when she had been left motherless at a young age. Her uncle, a surgeon in a Salonika clinic, was married to an Italian, a real signora. He often brought his wife bouquets of flowers for different occasions. My mother knew what to do with the flowers. She had a blue vase, rescued when they abandoned their house by the lake, that she had brought from Italy during the only trip with her husband she ever took. In the last move, she had taken the vase, a remembrance of that distant trip, together with a catalogue of the fashion house *La Rinascente* that showed spring fashions from some year in the nineteen-thirties. It was as if the vase, together with the flowers brought by Igor Lozinski, were from another era.

The evening grew into a beautiful holiday. Marija Hadjievski was there, happy, extremely happy, that she could help Mother and also be there with her boss, Igor Lozinski. She was happy that their house was a bridge connecting our family and Igor Lozinski.

Our old neighbor Vaskresija had also joined the preparations for the dinner. Her whole day had been spent by the charcoal oven baking her stuffed phyllo pies—putting them in, and baking them one after another—pies for which she was famous in the neighborhood and beyond. Mother was at her charcoal oven making *tikush*, pita with chicken. The smells of these creations—made with the skills from opposite shores of the lake—mingled. Who would think that between these tastes and smells was a border that could divide them? There was no border in that quiet Balkan night, in this happy region in the Balkan Babylon.

Kocho, pleased with his rich catch of the eels, yet not wishing to intrude on Father and Igor Lozinski's "plot," brought them a large eel prepared for roasting; it had been marinated in garlic, vinegar, and spices that, through some kind of Balkan alchemy, extracted all the bad fat. The remaining fat was baked away under the iron lid of the charcoal oven.

Kocho also brought wine that had been made from the grapes of his vineyards and stored for years in his cold cellar in anticipation of some special day, the day of liberation, or the day of Marija's engagement.

The scent of those wondrous foods spread to the river, blended with the fresh scent rising from the lake's waters, a scent drifting across even from his native shore, from the house of his birth.

Igor Lozinski, who was in obvious good spirits, began to sing a soft, nostalgic song. Father could not understand the words, but he felt the meaning of the pure and mournful beauty borne by the rhythm that had stolen upon the quiet. A few tears ran down Igor Lozinski's face. Then silence reigned once more.

There is a quiet that penetrates song and overcomes it. There now prevailed such a quiet, to which Father joined his song. From deep inside he drew out the sounds of Tosk polyphony. Late at night Kocho sometimes heard Father, who from the opened window of his library could be heard singing as if three voices were blending in continued succession, as if a trio were singing. Sometimes, there were, in fact, three singers, but sometimes Father sang alone. Old Kocho had a good ear, and he joined in the harmony that drifted from the neighboring house, from Father's library. Now as Father sang to his guests quietly, sound merging with the quiet, Kocho's voice could be heard.

Tears rolled down Father's face.

Igor Lozinski and Cvetan Gorski followed along with the song and then they quietly joined in. Such happiness had never before entered the house, nor had so many diverse songs, songs from both shores of the lake.

Chapter 14

After their unforgettable dinner, Father, Igor Lozinski, and Cvetan Gorski withdrew to the library. There, amid the opened books, maps, and illustrations of eels, was Mother's vase with Igor Lozinski's flowers. They scent was fresh despite the late autumn. Igor Lozinski's laboratory also boasted a small glass greenhouse, where he raised flowers, which at that time, everyone considered a true Balkan wonder.

The night was cold, quiet, starry. In the distance the drumbeats of the *tapan* marked the time of the last eels' departure. On the horizon, the lights of several torches flickered and then were lost to view, and the light from the low-hanging stars took over. There amid the books, Mother had lit the golden lamp — that good, merciful star in our house: a worthy, serene, and constant star shining in our exile.

Father and his two guests acted as if this were their last evening together. Each would then yield to his own fate. Each would follow his destiny along the path of the eels. They formed a small group of Balkan Don Quixotes. Whereas others were involved in the intricacies of how best to profit in these dark and uncertain times, these three were carried away by the path of the eels, and in their lofty goals, they were marginalized and misunderstood; they were incapable of grasping the trap that awaited as this new era unfolded.

Beside the desk-chair, in a prominent place, was Father's globe, on which was marked — following Igor Lozinski's model — the path of the eels from the lake to the distant Sargasso Sea. The whole world could be seen on this globe he'd purchased in Constantinople, all the names written in the new Latin orthography that Ataturk had introduced. Father had begged Igor to mark the path he had taken in following the eels from the Baltic Sea, extending along the Russian rivers, and arriving in the Balkans. Special markings designated Father's exit route from the Balkans to America, following the path of the eels.

Igor Lozinski occupied his usual place at the big table. He set down new books, drawings, and notes that neither Father nor Cvetan Gorski knew about. He was a strong man, with a large but tormented heart. Yes, his heart had matured; it had grown through the great suffering in his life. He had endured everything that the soul imagines exile to be. The arc of his exile, extending from the Baltic Sea to this lake in the southern Balkans, was long and filled with abundant uncertainties and traps, leading between life and death. He lived two, three lives in one. He had created a museum dedicated to the lake. He had clearly marked out the path of the eels from the lake to the ocean and back. He had even made models of the weirs. The weight of years had taken their toll. His life was passing by, with his dreams still not fully realized.

He had drawn close to Father at their first meeting. Although they came from opposite ends of fate in their exile, and their lives had differences, they had become like brothers. The interwoven fugue of great suffering that filled their souls had brought them close.

Now Igor Lozinski had come here among Father's books for a special confession, which he would also make before his great friend and his loyal student, the inheritor of his dreams. The lives of Father and Igor Lozinski were intersecting and separating at a true juncture of life's transience.

Igor Lozinski was first to break the silence.

"We have gathered tonight for a significant meeting," he said. "I must reveal to you the anguish that is gnawing at me. My days are numbered."

Father looked at his friend in surprise. Cvetan Gorski also couldn't hide his concern. Before they could say anything, Igor Lozinski continued.

"I am dying calmly. The lake has become my fatherland. And I discovered you, my friends, by this lake. We have joined our fates. Yet you have surely guessed the reason I have gathered you here; it is because of the future of the lake. Momentous change is coming."

There was silence.

Both Father and Cvetan Gorski wanted to say something in response to Igor's statement, but he suddenly continued.

"My friends, in these regions that are truly a gift of God, man will prove his greatness, his mettle, only in relation to the purity and longevity of the lake."

Speaking in this quiet manner, Igor Lozinski looked through the open window. All was silent. There are moments of silence that are more powerful than speech. These were such moments.

"It is by saving the purity of the lake that renews the freshwater springs that people can calmly await a new day," Igor Lozinski continued.

For a moment, Father and Cvetan Gorski could not figure out where their friend was headed with these thoughts. They had many ideas, but neither wanted to interrupt his flow of ideas.

"The fall of Fascism is coming. It has greatly muddied the waters of the lake and relations between people."

In his own way, Father continued to study the changes that had occurred in relations between people and the lake during those times when Balkan empires collapsed and he had a clear vision of the events that were unfolding, especially in regard to the impending fall of Fascism. However, his point of view focused on the significance of these events as they related to the family's safety and rested on a simple question: should they stay or should they go?

Igor Lozinski had a clearer understanding of the future. The arc of his European exile was greater than Father's. He clearly saw the triumph of Stalinism following its victory over Fascism. Igor Lozinski had to be trusted and Father and Cvetan Gorski listened to him attentively.

"In the new era, whichever regime comes to power will demonstrate its greatness through its relation to the lake. The lake must be kept clean, translucent, blue. Just as God created it millions of years ago. God forbid that the new regime should order river currents to be reversed to spill back into the lake.

Father and Cvetan Gorski were still not completely sure where Igor Lozinski was going, but he continued on clearly and directly.

"Let us hope that some Balkan neo-Stalinist does not take it into his head to build a hydroelectric station on one of the rivers that flows from the lake," he said.

"And block the path of the eels!" Cvetan Gorski immediately interrupted him.

"Exactly, my dear Gorski, and block the path of the eels!"

Cvetan Gorski said nothing.

"The end of Fascism is clear," continued Igor Lozinski. "They carried out a reign of terror. Fascism will surely be defeated; it cannot be saved. Communism, enraptured with its victory, will surely spread. God grant that it not be with Stalin's face and that it not continue the fateful errors it has made everywhere it has ruled."

As he listened to Igor Lozinski describe how he imagined the future between the fall of the empire of Fascism and the reign of Stalinism that would also encompass this part of the Balkans, the fate of the lake and the people around it, as Igor Lozinski described the severing of the eternal path of the eels, Father was drawing comparisons, a way of thinking adopted during his great uprooting. First, he considered how to continue the path of the eels to America before it was cut off, and then how to continue his *History of the Balkans through the Collapse of Its Empires*. Indeed, while listening to Igor Lozinski, Father was thinking that the severing of the path of the eels was commensurate with the collapse of an empire.

In his thoughts it was clear, at least in regard to the continuity of power, that one totalitarianism passed into the next; here, as always, he sensed the institution of the Janissary guard, with its history from ancient times in the Balkans, from the Macedonian phalanxes to the Praetorian Guard of the Roman Empire. The Ottoman Empire then instituted its Janissary system and Janissary army, made up of Islamized Christians. The Janissary system was later seen in the Russian Empire, in the Tsar's renowned guard, the streltsy, and it would acquire new forms in the Soviet Empire.

In the pending fall of Fascism, Father could perceive the march of the empire of Stalinism, headed by the new Janissary, Stalin, to whom Igor Lozinski was now clearly alluding, and who, the Russian feared, would one day reach the shores of the lake. Father was never able to interpret fully the Janissary system, which was to him as fleeting and transitory as the eels on their great and uncertain path. The Janissary system was one of the major Balkan legacies represented in Father's multifaceted library.

As he listened to Igor Lozinski predict the coming dangers of Stalinism and the battle that would ensue against the eels and their eternal pathway if, God forbid, it were to reach the shores of the lake, Father pensively turned his gaze to the library shelf containing his books about Janissaries.

"My friends," continued Igor Lozinski, "the lake has its origins in the Pliocene period. It came into existence before man appeared on the planet. In Europe, there are no lakes or springs more crystalline. Nor are there creatures older than those that live in the waters of this lake. There dwell rare living lake fossils. It is the lake's very continuity that is sacred. Since its birth in the Pliocene period, there has been continuity in the life of the lake; its evolution has never been interrupted.

"The lake was not touched by geologic changes in the surrounding relief, where mountains rose, valleys plummeted, other lakes appeared and disappeared. Nor did the Ice Age leave a lasting mark on the lake. So, my dear friends, the unique continuity of its existence makes the lake a true living Atlantis, a refuge and promised land for precious living creatures, survivors of Pliocene fauna.

"For Europe and our planet, the lake is a gigantic museum in whose clear waters ancient living fossils are preserved. Cvetan Gorski, my friends, and I managed to create a miniature museum exhibition of the flora and fauna of the lake to remind future generations of both the immortality and the mortality of the lake and those who live by its shores."

Igor Lozinski, who had proven worthy of his historic mission to save people from dreaded malaria, was now inspiring a flood of interconnected thoughts in Father's mind. When he first listened to Igor Lozinski, Father was filled with pride in his strong belief that the lake was his true fatherland. Now, he thought, did the lake not belong to all humanity?

Father was particularly captivated by what Igor Lozinski had said about the everlasting continuity of life in the lake. This was the most aching question in his historical research while he was writing his *History of the Balkans through the Collapse of Its Empires*. He was struck by the great paradox here beside the lake: nature was ruled by something eternal, a singular continuity in life, while the history of his family and of the people around the lake unfolded with the greatest, the most unimaginable, discontinuity.

He had set himself the nearly mythic task of discovering possible correspondences between the explosion of life in nature and its equivalent in human history. He constantly compared this relationship in the examples that man and nature provided him, even as he sought a model for his own exit. Listening to Igor Lozinski talk first about the passing of the empires of Fascism and Stalinism and then about the natural history of the lake, he began to realize more and more the truth that, in essence, Balkan history was beginning where it should have ended. But Balkan history most often failed to reach a conclusion; it was too entangled in relations with neighboring and other countries. It had to live with more history than could be endured.

In the quiet night that deepened into a feeling of eternity, the three friends did not notice that they had moved far beyond the eels, the topic that had brought them together. Both Father and Cvetan Gorski were lost deep in their own thoughts. The rich, powerful ideas expressed by Igor Lozinski continued on into the night that seemed to deepen without end.

Chapter 15

Listening to Igor Lozinski speak passionately of the lessons of his life story, Father thought foremost about the future of the Balkans and of European borders. Here, too, the eels entered his thoughts. They provided one more model from the natural world that humans should adopt, but could not.

What had Fascism accomplished? It had once again pitted one group against another; it had multiplied and shifted borders and had inflicted more suffering on the people. The Balkans was most cursed along those ideology-carved borders. Fascism had done this first, and now Stalinism threatened to do more. After all, hadn't Stalin dispersed peoples, changed alphabets, imposed new borders, all in the name of a new borderless universalism? New borders imposed on the old would merely add new twists in the Balkan labyrinths.

So now, before a new labyrinth formed, Father was determined to find an exit from the old one. Igor Lozinski's story drew him again to one possible path of escape: follow the eels on their migratory path toward America before the victors dreamt up new borders.

Poor victors, Father thought while listening intently, with the intuition of one who has been uprooted, to his friend's prediction that Stalinism could take hold even on the shores of the lake. Were it to do so, both the people and the eels would certainly suffer, as would the continuity of the natural world around the lake. A new border would once again divide the lake. It would divide the lake with all its living fossils. And in these thoughts about the approaching uncertain days, the eel slipped again into Father's mind, calling him to set off on the great journey.

The eel signaled a new stage in Father's exile. In that cursed Europe that was anticipating new borders, walls arose dividing nations, dividing faiths. Even in this period when the borders of Europe were being invaded, when the Soviets were approaching, the eels continued unimpeded on their circular path across the globe. The European eel continued its ancient fugue, its eternal flight, along a path begun before the dawn of humankind. Their pathway displayed the harmony of nature; it was a wondrous negation of the concept of borders, a negation of the new borders that man had established.

While he listened to Igor Lozinski discuss the possibility that Stalinism could reach the shores of the lake and erect new borders, reinforce old ones, and erect barriers to human hope, Father imagined himself, as in a dream, with his family moving ahead of the eels on a path to America. While thinking of this, he also imagined the crisscrossing of every conceivable border erected by humans and the manner in which the pathway of the eels erased those borders.

The road that led to America was always to be our family's direction. Most often, nearly always, it was a one-way trip. The traces of our family were lost forever in the American horizon. But now, seeing the eels' strong instinct for return it was finally possible to accept America as a destination in the family exile.

Father was alone with this important decision. It was clear to him that we always carried within us our own destiny, in which all possible borders and all possible escapes from those borders are inscribed. He was also aware in those moments that the natural world has neither history nor borders, that it lives only through established continuities. He reflected on how man betrayed what was natural in him through a belief in objective history. He believed that human happiness resided only on the white background of the pages of his books; the writing on those pages presented an unfaithful history.

Did not the borders themselves represent history? Was it the case that man would be happy only when he could find himself outside history, when he had freed himself of borders? In such moments, he wished to corroborate his thoughts with recollections from his endless reading. At times, he was ruled by the belief that history was essentially an attempt to realize the dream of freedom, to reach a perfect internal political order. At other times, seen from a Balkan perspective, history appeared to him a discontinuous whole. When he saw how Igor Lozinski coped with his own history, Father gathered evidence for his belief that history does not conquer those strong individuals who are able, at the price of great suffering and endurance, to look into the past in order to predict the future. While Father was contemplating his ideas on borders in the new era, Igor Lozinski was driven — on this stormy Balkan night dedicated to the salvation of the path of the eels — by the oracle of the past to look toward the future.

How could Father lead the family boat through the surging waters along the path of the eels from the lake into the ocean? How could he find the true exit to America, one possible route to salvation?

In the course of his studies of Balkan empires and their decline and fall, Father had focused most intently on the borders of the Ottoman Empire. In his quest for an exit from his Balkan impasse, he attempted first to isolate, then generalize — through the concept of paradigm — a model of empire, and from there, a single experience of empires.

The major empires, driven by a compulsion to dominate an ever expanding territory, left those within their borders fatally united by their differences, sharing a single idea of salvation, and therefore, tolerant of one another. They forgot boundaries; they had faith in one another and were accepting of their differences in language, food, and traditions. That is how it had been in the great Ottoman Empire, on which Father was considered to be an expert.

But now in this half-century in which Europe had been reshaped and borders had become more rigid, the eels were pushing him toward America, toward the new empire that opposed the Soviets, who were taking their place among the new victors. Father firmly believed that, with each victory, new Janissaries were created. Each empire, not only in the Balkans but also throughout the world, owed its rise and fall to the glory and the misery of the enduring institution of the Janissary.

Father had determined that he would select one of the two rising empires: the American or the Soviet. He was certain that the family's identity would be threatened in either option; it would be altered forever, something that had not happened in the long five centuries of the Ottoman Empire. Following the natural paradigm, the path of the eels that had still not been closed, Father was determined to take the path to America. The books he had read in an order that seemed to him most appropriate, pointed him in that direction. The choice of America meant a choice for that open expanse and in support of his belief that our strength increases in exile. America offered him a final horizon where he could forge his family's destiny. Choosing to remain in Europe, with little luck, meant a choice for the vertical dimension, further service to its history and entanglement in its continuities.

This is what Father contemplated by his open books during that stormy Balkan night, while the eels — reduced in number by the multitude caught by fishermen and trapped in weirs — continued on their way to America.

Chapter 16

In that dark Balkan night, the three friends shared their common utopian dream: what would happen to the eels, those poor eels, if Stalinism did in fact reach the shores of the lake and take root in the souls of the people?

For Father, the question about the future of the eels and their eternal path was, in fact, a question about the future of the people, those whose fate had caused them to flee, those who shared the same fate as his family. He had begun to realize that no creature besides the eel had a life cycle that unfolded across such a vast expanse of the planet.

For both Cvetan Gorski — who was preparing to dedicate his life to saving the eels and to uncovering the secret of their pathway — and Father — who was discovering a possible escape route from his exile by following the eels — Igor Lozinski's discoveries had a transformative effect on their lives.

This Russian emigrant who had discovered in the lake a true Fatherland, wanted — through his discovery of the mystic path of the eels and his work for its survival — to send a final message both to those living in this region and to all humanity. While Father and Cvetan Gorski listened to the inimitable Igor Lozinski, each continued, driven by his own inner motives, to imagine following the enigmatic path of the eels that their friend had revealed to them.

Millions of eels from lakes everywhere, from unknown, calm waters, set off that dark Balkan night, on their great and uncertain path, to the rhythm of life's impermanence; they set off toward the ocean of their death and resurrection. And in Father's mind, there also continued the endless march of millions of people, carried by their dream to set off toward new shores of salvation when the suffering caused by Fascism pressed and threatened.

People were departing for regions without history so they could pull their lives from meaninglessness and pass on what remained of those lives to new generations. From the most remote places on the planet, driven by mystical forces or by some genetic code imprinted at birth, this living protoplasm flowed together, seeking sources for its renewal.

For Father, who continued to seek a way out of his exile through a return to his native land, the *return* of the eels through a new generation was especially attractive; here was a possible paradigm provided in the natural world, whose significance man had somehow forgotten, that of a lost paradise. What a wondrous solution for squaring the circle of life!

The line of a powerful flash of lightening illuminated the sky above the lake, followed by the loud rolling thunder, shattering the gathered quiet above its waters. When the sky grew calm again, Igor Lozinski was first to speak.

"Science is today unable to explain the riddles of the eels' heroic path. Now, even on this stormy night, the eels are streaming along the turbulent waters. It is likely that the storm combined with the magnetic currents it creates are somehow connected to the general order that streams to the eels, a call to begin their great journey. This journey — both heroic and ascetic — leads to their inevitable death."

The holy books in Father's library were placed between his books about Janissaries and his Balkan bestiaries, most of which were about eels and goats. As he listened to Igor Lozinski, Father looked vaguely toward the holy books, as if seeking help from those pressed between the eels and the Janissaries. More to himself than the others, he quietly whispered, "Because of these pathways, unexplored and not yet fully explained, religions arise, followed by arbitrary ideologies, until scientific truth — which often remains beyond man's grasp — prevails."

Igor Lozinski looked tenderly at Father. His expression showed he understood this reasoning, even though it led his thoughts in a different direction, and he spoke again, glancing toward Cvetan Gorski.

"My friends," he said. "I am tormented by something else when discussion is about the eels and their migratory routes. That is why I came here to see you, my brothers in fate, to open my heart to you, to tell you about my final worries before my life ends."

Father looked at his companion with surprise and was overcome by a great sadness. What sort of role could Igor Lozinski imagine for him when he knew his powerlessness as an immigrant? After all, wasn't Igor Lozinski himself an immigrant? Oh, how many times harder his migration had been than Father's. Still, the trust that Igor Lozinski showed in him filled him with courage and gave him faith that he could accomplish something more significant than he, an immigrant, could ever have imagined.

There was another flash above the lake. A long, bright, jagged line cut across the sky. This bolt of lightening cut the sky, illuminating the lake above the invisible border dividing the two countries. When quiet returned, Igor Lozinski continued.

"My friends," he said, "I have come to love these people, these nations living around the lake. I have loved them with all the differences and contradictions that have always separated them, but never severed them completely. I loved these people, just as I loved the plants and animals living in and around the lake. These waters, these crystalline waters, which originated long ago in the distant Cenozoic era, many, many years before the dawn of humanity, have maintained the balance between mankind and nature, and they have maintained the balance in the people themselves. Farther from the lake, men seemed more easily to get caught up in battles, suffer greater defeats, but here, peace and humanity have prevailed.

"Here, as nowhere else in the Balkans, here in this lake region, man has maintained a balance with life. Thousands, millions of years have passed, yet man, despite all his burdens and suffering, has remained faithful to the lake and to the life it contains: the eels, the trout, the sponges and microorganisms, to all the animals here in nature's sanctuary. But after everything I have seen and endured, with Stalin at my heels, both in my homeland and in exile here at the lake, my final fatherland, I am pursued by fear. God forbid, God forbid."

Igor Lozinski fell silent. At that moment, Mother entered the room. She brought tea prepared in the Balkan samovar, tea that pushed away sleep and cleared the mind. When she heard Igor Lozinski's last words directed to God, she thought of the worst, of war — what else? Father sensed her disquiet; he caressed her with the blue of his eyes that could penetrate souls, and she left, calmed.

Igor Lozinski sipped his tea, nodded in pleasure, and continued.

"You know, my friends, I traveled a great distance to get here, from the far reaches of the Russian landmass. I will tell you that even as a young man on the shore of the Baltic, I was caught up in the great riddle of the path of the eels. I don't know myself how it came to captivate me. They led me along their path. And that has lasted to the end of my life. I lived with the hope that I would uncover the meaning of their circular travel as a kind of immortality. But now the twilight of my life is at hand."

Father stared into Igor Lozinski's eyes, the source of his soul. As his friend pronounced those last words, two, three tears ran down his face, adding power to the significance of what he was saying. Then he went on.

"Oh, those eels, those blessed and cursed eels, like sirens of the northern seas they entered the rivers and lakes of our Russian land; they bound me to the world; they outlined countless escape routes at a time when human beings were being suffocated by their fate."

Father recognized in Igor Lozinski's words some of what he had been thinking. With impatience, he waited for him to continue, hoping that his words would fully illuminate his own thoughts.

"I calmly began to study the path of the eels," Igor Lozinski continued, "after reading all the literature about their migration. While I was studying at the Military Medical Academy in Petersburg and later, during my specialization, I never stopped studying the eels and their migration paths. Many people wondered, but no one understood why I had become so engrossed with the subject. No one cared to try to understand the reasons for my search.

"My friends, I harbored at that time the secret idea of following the path of the eels — as you do now — to stay ahead of uncertain times, using it as a possible escape and salvation from my own people. At that time, my dear friends, disastrous events were on the horizon. It was clear that in the wake of the French revolution — the 'worm' of progress would continue to eat away at our planet. Progress in itself is understandable, but when its message is manipulated, when ideologies are grafted onto it, misfortune is the logical consequence."

Where was Igor Lozinski now heading? Father asked himself. When he considered his Balkan point of view, he saw there was both logic and truth in what his friend was saying. Father waited impatiently to see what direction his thoughts would take.

"In history it is not the misfortune or the catastrophe that is the worst, but it is the error, the huge mistake equivalent to stupidity, that leads to catastrophe and misfortunes. When that mistaken idea is taken as truth, it moves more rapidly to destruction than mere catastrophe. A misfortune can be overcome, but the mistaken idea remains, providing the opportunity for that misfortune to be repeated. It was in error, for example, that Lenin decided to 'copy' the French revolution and transfer it to Russia."

Father had a natural propensity to accept these general ideas; he had an ear for their chimerical reverberation, particularly when he was writing his *History of the Balkans through the Collapse of Its Empires*. In Igor Lozinski's narrative he saw how one ordinary error, an error in the mind of Lenin, incited the fall of the Tsarist Russian Empire and gave rise to the Soviet Empire, which would surely one day experience its apotheosis and fall with Stalinism. Even though he felt that the discussion was moving away from the theme of the eels and their paths of migration, Father followed the flow of his friend's thoughts with great interest.

"And so, my dear friends, Lenin's mistakes were compounded by the new ones Stalin committed. The irony of fate! Stalin compounded Lenin's mistakes just as Lenin, at the end of his life, had become aware of them and their catastrophic consequences. That's how it is in the history of mankind and of the world. Errors have determined history. Hitler, too, founded his empire on a mistaken idea. The premise of the domination of one race has led to catastrophes of planetary dimensions. One error gives birth to new ones. Stalin has triumphed in the battle of those who commit such errors, my friends. But now, emboldened by his victory over Fascism, he will continue to commit new errors."

Igor Lozinski's prediction was clear. The wave of mistakes would swell to a tsunami if it also reached the shores of the lake. To Father, it was as clear as day where Igor Lozinski's thoughts were heading, even though they were moving far beyond the main topic for which they had gathered that evening.

"But, to return to the path of the eels," continued Igor Lozinski, "and how they, too, became victims of Stalin's error. This same mistake threatens the eels in the lake as well."

But when? How? These were the things Father and Cvetan Gorski wanted to hear from Igor Lozinski that night.

"Let me return to the path of the eels," Igor Lozinski said, "to the time when ideology divided the country into 'Reds' and 'Whites.' That division was settled in bloodshed. Many perished. Red blood darkened and was swept away in the rapid river currents. There were torrents of people leaving. Many dreams were cut short. Still the eels continued to travel down rivers reddened with spilled blood. But that was not the most terrible thing."

Igor Lozinski fell silent a moment. The storm had quieted. The old stars in the sky sparkled. Shafts of light illuminated the lake. Igor Lozinski was captivated by the source of this heavenly light spilling onto the lake, and he fixed his gaze on the lowest-hanging star. It surely reached the horizon of his native land. His land of no return.

There were still many, many twists for Igor Lozinski to unwind in his tormented and wounded soul before he could touch bottom, where the soul frees itself from all heaviness and hovers between life and death. He was ready to reveal the most terrible thing that had happened, either something in his life or in the life of his country. He quickly resolved this question.

"During that cursed period of Stalinism," he said, "someone discovered my secret search for the path of the eels. Those were dark times. Everyone informed on everyone. No one could possess a secret, even the smallest. They kept me and my study of eels under surveillance. It was all written down in a police dossier. I saved myself in whatever way I could. I traveled in search of the microorganisms that caused epidemics. I traveled across taigas, deserts, tundra. I survived.

"One night, a telegram caught up with me in distant Siberia: 'Comrade Igor Lozinski, you are called urgently to Moscow. A new mission awaits you!' The Central Committee had called me to a special commission that was in session in the Kremlin. They were focusing great attention on me, I told myself. But who knew whether for good or ill? I set off immediately for Moscow.

"'Comrade Lozinski, are you quite familiar with the Russian eels and their migrations? That is what is noted in your dossier,' they said, directing the Kremlin Commission's first question to me. 'Yes, Comrade President, I know the Russian eels well; I have been studying them for thirty years, but there are many things that are difficult to discover, particularly in regard to their migration. I am at your service,' I said, both anxious and confused.

"'You have been selected by the party to participate in the construction of the White Sea Canal,' the President told me in a peremptory tone. A cold shiver ran through my body. I felt at that moment both convicted and condemned. Rare is the man who returns alive from the White Sea Canal. In whatever capacity one went, there was no return. However, I composed myself. The fact that my mission was connected with the eels offered me a ray of hope. Following the path of the eels, I would have some chance of saving myself. But I still could not see what the purpose of my mission was."

Neither Father nor Cvetan Gorski had expected this turn in Igor Lozinski's narrative. Their friend poured himself some tea from the samovar and continued.

"So, my dear Balkan friends, at that moment in the Kremlin meeting, I could not determine why I was being sent to the Gulag. Whether it was on account of someone's petty revenge or because I was on the list of unfit and exploitative 'Whites' and my turn had come, I had no way of determining. I had no choice but to abandon myself to the fate that had been given me. And I set off…"

Chapter 17

As he listened to Igor Lozinski, Father imagined new pages turning in his *History of the Balkans through the Collapse of Its Empires*. Were the eels also to have some significance in establishing the empire of Stalinism in the Balkans? He commented out loud on Igor Lozinski's narrative concerning the apotheosis of Stalinism, more to himself, but still audible to the others, saying, "If the migratory route of the eels is broken, that will be a sign that here, too, Stalin's empire has begun its reign."

"That is right, my friend," Igor Lozinski replied, "if one follows the experience of Stalinism in relation to the eels. But, what will happen here is difficult to predict. There are some new developments that, perhaps, support this comparison."

This digression in Father's thoughts away from the main focus of Igor Lozinski's tale in fact increased his curiosity to learn more of the experience his Russian friend had endured under Stalinism, seeing it as a model of escape and salvation for the people and territories Stalin conquered. Father and Cvetan Gorski had only fragmentary knowledge of Stalin's pharaonic mania of sacrifice, stemming from Stalin's error. Stalin wished to connect the White Sea with the Baltic by building a canal in just ten years in order to catch up to the West, which, he believed, was about one hundred years ahead.

Here, as in his *History of the Balkans through the Collapse of Its Empires,* Father confronted the painful question of continuity and discontinuity in history. With their founding, the great empires sought to establish a new line of continuity with a new army. For Father, this was the clear continuation of the Janissaries. The powerlessness to discover true continuity, led in turn to the triumph of broken lines of development which strengthened the new victors' illusion that they could impose a false continuity, based on utopian principles, and claim that their's was the true, natural, continuity.

Stalin wanted to fill this vacuum, eliminate this abyss with great leaps, through the sacrifice of human lives in order to create a great and glorious future. This method took an obvious, classic form. It has been accomplished from the age of the Pharaohs up to the age of Stalinism and Maoism. In Father's view, it was no coincidence that at the head of this new project for the future strode a new dictator — the new Janissary Stalin.

Listening to Igor Lozinski discuss Stalin and his errors, Father thought of his typology of Balkan dictators — Janissaries who provoked the fall of their own empires. In Father's view, it was becoming clear that, here in the Balkans, the late arrival of Stalinism grafted onto the incomplete fall of the Ottoman Empire could give rise to even more serious consequences.

Igor Lozinski interrupted Father's thoughts just as he had reached an impasse.

"There was no limit to the insanity of Stalin's ideas to transform the country into a labyrinth. Not even the path of the eels was spared! But the order to build the White Sea Canal, intended to connect the White and Baltic Seas, was one of Stalin's greatest, most serious mistakes, bordering on madness. The grim 1930s were unfolding at the height of Stalinism in Russia. Without Lenin's critical mind or those of his supporters, Stalin set off on an all-or-nothing campaign toward the triumph of Communism, without considering the cost of the millions of human lives that would be sacrificed. First to pay were the kulaks. Industrialization at any cost was paramount. The limits of a planned economy were apparent. Defeat was inevitable. Stalin began to seek the 'devil' in the souls of the people. He discovered 'saboteurs'; a veritable campaign was waged against the builders. The agony of sacrifice stretched on."

Father listened and considered the origins of sacrifice and the cycles of sacrifice that sustained empires. Unable to build on the continuity of true progress or of old beliefs, they resorted to instruments of sacrifice that operated flawlessly only while the empires lasted. So it has been since the age of the Pharaohs up to these cursed times. Everything remained the same; only the forms of sacrifice were different.

"And in that euphoria of sacrifice, in the fight against 'saboteurs,' only a new victory — according to the mechanism governing the soul of a defeated Janissary — could compensate for defeat," Igor Lozinski continued. "Yes, according to the dislocated logic of the Janissary soul, those lagging behind must accelerate the process of catching up with those who are ahead, but always at the expense of new victims. And so Stalin hatched the crazy idea of building the White Sea Canal. In a different era, such a canal had been the dream of the Russian Tsar Paul I. But unlike Stalin, even that mad tsar had not dared to carry out the project."

Father found yet another proof in Igor Lozinski's words for his thesis that empires go to extreme measures, committing tremendous errors, when the price of their defeat must be paid for by the innocent lives of those who are sacrificed. That was how it had been with all the empires in the Balkans. He could give many examples that would add to his friend's theses, but he restrained himself.

No matter how far Father's thoughts wandered from Igor Lozinski's story of the White Sea Canal, he waited with anticipation for new information about the absurd construction of Stalin's pyramid of water. Father knew it could help him to escape history at this moment when Stalinism was threatening the Balkans from all sides and seeking a pathway toward new victims. Igor Lozinski seemed to guess his thoughts.

"So Stalin's most absurd orders began to be realized," he said, "to build the waterway that was to connect the Baltic Sea and the White Sea, passing through the Svir River, along Lake Ladoga, reaching the city of Povenets and then on to the extreme north, to the river Onega, where the White Sea Canal would then terminate in the port city of Belomorsk, at the very entrance to the White Sea.

"The canal had a total length of 227 kilometers, of which 37 were man-made canals connecting 190 kilometers of lakes and rivers. It had nineteen locks for regulating the level of water to permit navigation, forty-nine dikes, and fifteen dams. The ultimate goal in constructing the canal was to shorten the route between Saint Petersburg and Belomorsk by four thousand kilometers. In this game of numbers that would last until the canal's construction was complete, Stalin's strategic aim was to catch up to the West and surpass it, leaving out of the calculation the number of innocent victims, a number that would reach three hundred thousand. The graves those of innocent victims were never discovered. Of the thousands of former convicts, women, and children who worked on the canal, half had been convicted of 'counter-revolutionary activities.' The villagers, victims of forced collectivization, constituted the majority of the prisoners building the canal. Such is the irony of fate: their land was taken away, and they ended their lives in watery graves.

"Even more tragic was the fact that the construction of the entire length of the canal, more than two hundred kilometers, had to be completed within twenty months. It was hell on Earth. The land had to be leveled. Work was carried out in a frozen climate, in rocky terrain that had been untouched by shovels since the creation of Earth. Stalin's order specified that the canal would not cost a great deal. It would be an inexpensive construction project. This was a diabolical calculation. The labor cost nothing. Such 'free' labor would replace bulldozers and excavators. The hills would be leveled with bare hands; thousands of wheelbarrows would transform the land.

"And so Stalin, relying on man, and man alone, left those people with bare hands, like unlucky Sisyphus pushing the boulder to oblivion. With just a bit of machinery, many, many lives would have been saved. But who considered the people at that time? The stupidity increased; it was enormous. He began to think and to organize. Orchestras of reputed artists were found to hasten the construction, to raise morale. However, the music sounded more like a funeral march, sounding tragic-grotesque chords in this landscape of death."

Igor Lozinski stopped talking. Thunder reverberated again in the distance. Father and Cvetan Gorski must surely have asked themselves how this was possible and — of greatest interest to them — what had been the fate of the canal and what role Igor Lozinski had played in it. He picked up their thoughts.

"In the end," he said, "the White Sea Canal was neither deep enough nor navigable enough. The failure was obvious, but it had to be celebrated as if it were a triumph. Again, the stupidity continued. New orchestras arrived, respected artists and writers, all given the task to portray black as white. The writers must demonstrate that the building of the canal had led to the moral salvation of the convicts as well."

As he listened, Father could see clearly the long reach of the stupidity and blindness of a dictator obsessed with the idea of creating a new rhythm for his empire through the total sacrifice of his subjects — all in order to compete with the more rapid tempo of that other empire. It was clear from Igor Lozinski's tale that Stalinism's ultimate goal, through its vast system of sacrifice seen in the construction of the White Sea Canal, was to catch up to the Euro-American tempo of progress.

Stalin, Father thought, did not realize that he had, in fact, succeeded only in hastening the sacrifice of innocent citizens for his empire. To Father, it was once again made clear that he must follow the path of the eels before he was imprisoned.

Chapter 18

Igor Lozinski's dramatic retelling of the tragedy of the construction of the White Sea Canal in far-off Russia deeply disturbed Father and Cvetan Gorski. But the story the Russian had told them also helped them both in their individual quests. For Father, Igor Lozinski's evidence was of major significance in his ongoing research for his *History of the Balkans through the Collapse of Its Empires*. His ideas also provided fertile ground for the scientific imagination of his faithful student Cvetan Gorski, who was now engaged more than ever before in the future of the lake's eels. He understood the great importance the eel had for the fauna of this ancient lake.

While Cvetan Gorski listened to his teacher, he thought how the tragedy of the workers who built the White Sea Canal also signified a tragedy for the northern Russian eel, for the billions of creatures inhabiting the northern rivers and lakes that became victims of that unforeseen alteration in their habitat. Human error changed their biological rhythms. Here, too, among the first to suffer would be the eels and their circular path across the planet.

It was clear that Igor Lozinski's narrative indicated the possibility that Stalinism, through the creation of a separate small Balkan gulag, would block forever the path of the eels living here. Cvetan Gorski could imagine how the new regime's mistakes and stupidity would arise. The analogy and allusion flowing from his teacher's narrative were quite clear: there would likely be a break in the path of the eels through construction of a local variant of the Russian White Sea Canal adapted to this river — the eels' watery bridge between the lake and the ocean. And who would consider the eels' route then?

In the name of progress, life itself would be destroyed. That is what Cvetan Gorski thought as he listened, impatient to hear the full story of Igor Lozinski's experience with the disruption of the path of the Baltic eels at the height of Stalinism so he could grasp more clearly the fate of the eels living here in the lake.

Igor Lozinski was aware of his student's great curiosity. Without being asked, he continued.

"What more can I tell you? I was assigned the task of studying the response of the living world around the White Sea Canal: of the rivers, lakes, and seas, and wherever living creatures — known and unknown — had lived there, from before the time of man to the present. For a scientist, there may be no greater dream than to explore this living, surging universe of life. But it turned out differently. First, I had to fulfill my work quota. To tell the truth, I dug less than the others. The rest of the time, I worked in my laboratory, where I collected all kinds of specimens of the organisms living in those northern waters.

"I had to submit reports concerning these microscopic creatures, while all around me, silently or shouting condemnation and cursing Stalin's empire, people were dying. And when the construction of the White Sea Canal was completed, it was as if a hell on Earth had been completed. More people perished than survived. Because they were prisoners, the survivors had to return to prison. However, Stalin took pity on them and freed them. Those wretched people who had worked on the canal had already suffered the greatest punishment.

"But my mission at the White Sea Canal did not end then. I had to submit both a report and samples of the river, lake, and sea fauna, with data concerning their survival and evolution in the new canal. The samples of fauna I selected to present as evidence to the scientific institutes in Moscow and Saint Petersburg were few in number compared with the thousands of people who had perished. They studied my reports for weeks, months, years, but I was never summoned for discussion or deposition. The White Sea Canal was not navigable, nor was it suitable for any other use, and it remained caught in a web of oblivion.

"In all the years I spent researching the areas around the construction of the White Sea Canal, the migration of the eels held my wakeful attention. But whom could I interest at that time in the path of the eels, since it found itself in the same labyrinth from which people, too, could not escape?"

"In other words, the migration path of the eels was compromised by the construction of the White Sea Canal?" Cvetan Gorski asked after a long time.

"That is how it is, my dear friend Gorski," Igor Lozinski quickly replied. "Sins against man and his life are also sins against nature."

"But what happened to the eels?" Father asked, seeking clarification even though the answer had already been given.

"The eels turned about in a circle. They did not get to the fresh water of the rivers and lakes at the right time to continue their primordial mission of life and death. Nor did the eels return to the seas."

"And what happened to you and your work at the institute in Saint Petersburg?" Cvetan Gorski asked.

"I was then subjected to new torments. They were not pleased with my report. The chapter about the eels, no matter how discretely it was put, held a secret, a certain mystique that was not in line with party views of proletarian science. Who knew what punishment I would be given? Had I been a member of the party, they would have dealt with me easily. Of course, one could not be a 'White' and a member of the party. I was given a final warning before being excluded from the institute. They knew quite well that they still needed my expertise as an authority on parasitic microorganisms.

"Well enough, but I was consumed by anxiety. I resolved to follow the path of the eels. I would head south, following the rivers, just as the eels had formerly traveled from the sea to the lakes. I followed the imagined path of the eels. Somewhere, there had to be a way out! The eels revealed the invisible watery borders that united Europe. There had to be a way out somewhere! The migratory route of the eels had not been cut everywhere. And so, my dear Balkan friends, I reached this lake, my final fatherland. Here I have lived a new life. The life that was taken from me in my native Russia was returned to me here."

Father was completely engrossed in Igor Lozinski's incomparable narrative. He would readily have compared his quest for the path of the eels with Igor Lozinski's, but that was impossible. Each person had his own unique path in life. Even so, these two who had been so forcibly uprooted were joined in a fugue of flight, suffering, and faith. Father, too, believed that following the eels would lead him and his family at last to the promised land, to the Atlantis of a peaceful life.

What a planetary paradox: Father was fleeing from the lake in search of an exit from exile from the place where Igor Lozinski had found salvation and peace, his own exit from exile. Father traveled, seeking an exit along the pathway of the eels in the opposite direction from the path that had led Igor Lozinski to Father's native lake, where he had discovered a new fatherland.

The sky above the lake had filled with stars, as if it were celebrating the salvation of the eels along their migratory path to the sea. Father's hopes survived with those eels and now traveled with them, first across the border with the neighboring country, then to the sea, and the ocean, marking one variation of possible return.

In the distance, the first red rays of sunrise were breaking through. The blue water of the lake surrendered to its metamorphosis, hastened by the appearance of the sun. The city still slept, dreaming of the eels streaming toward the sea.

Father, Igor Lozinski, and Cvetan Gorski, unnoticed by Mother, went out of the house and set off toward the river and the lake, just then awakening, its depths stirring with thousands of living organisms, those last surviving living fossils, which seemed to greet their saviors.

Chapter 19

Father, Igor Lozinski, and Cvetan Gorski were bound to this lake and to its history. Indeed, the lake had a history, a great history. Deep in its womb, the lake held mythic roots in which peoples' destinies were entangled.

Igor Lozinski wanted to finish his great confession to his Balkan friends, to tell them the secrets he had uncovered studying the continuity of life in the lake and the people inhabiting its shores. He wanted to pass on to Cvetan Gorski a moral testament and the hope that his work and desire for truth would continue, and he wished to reveal something of greater significance to Father in his ongoing quest to find an escape from exile along the path of the eels.

When they paused at the spot where the river flows from the lake, where the slow and rapid waters mix and where the impermanence of things quickened, the sky in the east was already turning red, and the eye of the sun was greeting the blue waters. The water flowed quietly from the lake. It was the end of twilight and a wondrous calm reigned at the very dawning of the day. Along the surface of the blue water, two white swans approached from the distance like the first rays of the awakening lake. Igor Lozinski gazed at the rapid waters of the river flowing from the lake and was the first to break the silence.

"During all of life's painful moments," he said, "I have calmed myself beside rapid waters. And now my life is ending here by these slow waters, which seem to slow even the transient nature of things."

Igor Lozinski was moving toward a new melancholic narrative, which would lead him once more toward the truth, a truth that drew his friends closer and then pushed them away.

"I have already told you, my friends," Igor Lozinski said quietly, "that I sense I do not have much life left to follow the current of these waters and the fate of these eels toward their great pathway to the ocean and await their return."

His message was clear: Igor Lozinski still had something dramatic to say, something he had to dig from the depths of his soul. He was silent a long time; the quiet rippling of the indigo waters of the river guarded the quiet. Finally, he spoke.

"This river flows away from the Balkans, linking with the Sea and then the Atlantic Ocean. That is how it has been for hundreds, thousands, millions of years, since before the appearance of man. The first forms of life, long before humans, inhabited this lake. Many have endured as living fossils. It is the eels alone that are fated to complete a circular path, to connect the fresh waters and salt waters of our planet.

"And when human life arrived in this region, the eels continued to follow their migratory route, marking their life cycle. And as human knowledge matured, humankind confronted inexplicable truths, and then legends arose and were passed on, legends that included the eels. There were deities for whom the eels became messengers. The eels have outlived the pharaohs, emperors, dictators; no borders or boundaries could halt their path. And as you see, my friends, the eels have survived up to the fateful Stalinist era."

Father and Cvetan Gorski, each with his own vantage point, knowledge, and assumptions, were deeply engrossed in the epic course of Igor Lozinski's thoughts, but neither could see clearly where it would end.

"The end of Fascism is approaching," their friend continued. "One can also sense the end of this empire of nationalist evils. I fear that the enchantment of victory will not last long, and the victors will end in defeat. Here by the lake, Stalinism will mix up many things. God grant that his mad schemes will not be repeated, those plans that displace waters and peoples, as happened in Russia. May God also grant that in our quest for light — light created by dams and hydroelectric stations on the river — no one will think to interrupt the path of the eels."

Igor Lozinski fell silent. The cry of the lake gulls could be heard. The sun had already spread across the blue waters that now sparkled in new, unexpected streams of blueness. These last words — the message Igor Lozinski passed on to them — became firmly etched in the memory of both Father and Cvetan Gorski. Those words contained a hint of the future as well. Neither Father nor Cvetan Gorski would realize that in that moment they were hearing the final words of their great friend and teacher, Igor Lozinski.

As the sun set on Fascism and dawned on Stalinism, Igor Lozinski vanished forever. Although these were hard times of war, his many friends arranged a burial worthy of him. Stronger than all else, his memory continued to live in the souls of those he had saved from malaria and other diseases. The entire animal kingdom of the great lake and the life around it lost its great scholar, friend, and savior. His museum, dedicated to that life, was preserved for posterity, giving testimony not only to his work, but also to the continuity of life within and around the lake. There had never been a greater Balkan institution than the museum created by Igor Lozinski to bear witness to such a long era and with such details of the lake's continuity. Millions of years in the lake's history were represented in the museum exhibit.

A central place in the collection was held by an exhibit of the migration route of the eels, from the lake to the Sargasso Sea and back, with a model of a weir, complete with eels caught during their departure and return, each phase of their migration clearly marked. A whole kingdom of creatures had been stuffed and mounted in order to bear witness forever to their majestic existence; they were there for the times that were coming, a time filled with insecurity for the people, the lake, and the creatures, known and unknown, that inhabited it.

Igor Lozinski's great soul had spread good works wherever it touched those suffering torment or pain in the lake region. A monument was erected in his honor: a stone bird with a broken wing, which recalled his years of exile. But while he was alive, he had built his own enduring monument in the souls of those who suffered. Igor Lozinski's collection outlived the occupation and the war.

The one most responsible for saving his collection was Cvetan Gorski, who, during the years of Fascism, managed together with Igor Lozinski's close relatives to protect the valuable exhibits and, after the war, to preserve them in a museum unique to the Balkans and the world. But it was not easy. Cvetan Gorski felt an immeasurable heaviness weighing on his spirit during the first days of Stalinism. How could he praise the work of Igor Lozinski, a White Guard, at a time when the Red Army was clearing everything in its path? And who was to be swept away first? The White Guards, "those damned class traitors," — certain victims of the victorious ideology.

In those difficult and uncertain times, Cvetan Gorski wondered whether Igor Lozinski' s soul was so big, powerful, long-suffering, and perceptive that it had quietly disappeared just ahead of the possibility of a new encounter with Stalinism.

But death can also occur as the natural culmination of a life filled with greatness and suffering, a life whose mission is passed on to someone else. At the moment when the web of Stalinism was spreading across the lake, Cvetan Gorski fought heroically from the very first days to save the collection of lake flora and fauna created by his teacher and spiritual father.

It was difficult in those days to think about, let alone openly defend, the work of Igor Lozinski. But it was also impossible that this great lake and river of eternal departure could not temper the new strident tone and severe, implacable apparatchiks of the Stalin reign — no matter how strong the inertia created by its ideological propaganda. At least not when Igor Lozinski's work was in question.

Chapter 20

Igor Lozinski's absence brought Father and Cvetan Gorski closer. The vivid memory of their friend, the fulfillment of his moral will and the multifaceted tasks he left to them became a living bridge between them.

Although new sufferings had now begun to torment Father as Stalinism was implanted in his native land as well as in the land of his exile — countries divided by an ostensibly open and fraternal border — he did not fall into the trap of hasty return; his exile had deep roots. He sensed that he had to move ahead of history. In his mind, return to his native land meant to step back, behind history. Here, too, lay the path of the eels.

As he waited for the first years of Stalinism, Father decided to remain awhile in the town where the river flows from the lake. He wanted to see first what would happen with the path of the eels, whether Igor Lozinski's prediction would come true. In his own way, he also wanted to help Cvetan Gorski, if a hand were raised against the river and the eels. He wanted to see what the outcome of Stalinism would be in his nearby native land.

His forebodings seemed to be materializing. Across the lake, Stalinism had grafted onto fertile soil. Tribal instinct for power — unabated with the fall of the Ottoman Empire — made all evolution difficult. The Stalinist regime took root more deeply there than anywhere else, and through the ambitions of new Stalinists, this regime would survive longer there than in the country of its birth. The country was closed, cemented in, borders erected like walls. The border that divided Father from his close kin, one hour as a bird flies, separated the people on the two shores of the lake, as if they now lived on two separate planets.

But here where the river flowed from the lake, Stalinism governed for two tumultuous years until the feud between Tito and Stalin; after Tito's courageous "No," Stalinism quietly vanished from this land by the lake, even though its inertia continued. While in Father's native land it thrived, finding suitable soil in the prevailing mentality of those in power, here the inertia would continue through rapid creation of what the Soviets called the "New

Man," with the inherited Stalinist illusion that one could make up for lost time through the forced construction of projects that were not feasible.

Father's choice between two borders was between the Stalinism that would slowly disappear on one side and the Stalinism that would experience a monstrous resurrection on the other side. On both sides of the border, the path of the eels was threatened. Father needed either to follow them while there was still time or choose a third path for our family.

As a lawyer naturally in opposition to the regime in power, Father had done much good on both sides of this lake that divided two countries along shifting borders, and he could now more realistically than before hope to find an escape for his family: either return to his native land or continue his path of exile. But Father — atavistically entranced by the route of the eels, as if driven by some divine portent inscribed in that path and in Igor Lozinski's prediction — ultimately decided to head north, to follow the eels as far as possible.

The Constantinopolitan star that had shone during his youth and, later, in his dreams to move his family eastward had slowly extinguished over time. The strong family inclination not to lose its lakeside identity remained. But the path of the eels toward the north, toward the sea — which offered a possible way out together with the longed-for *return* — depended on new historical events. It was clear to him that Stalinism, in the euphoria of its victory over Fascism, had not, in its first years, bared its true teeth to the Balkans, even though here were many obedient wolves ready to help it endure.

The arrow in Father's soul, his compass, quivered a long time, then directed him northwestward, as long, that is, as the path of the eels survived. Either that, or he needed to find a different exit from the Balkans, following the course of a different river. New events would set Father's course away from the town where the river flowed from the lake. The country that had been created after the war, in which Father had for some time held the status of an immigrant, provided him the opportunity to have two fatherlands: one at the republic level, Macedonia, the other at the state level, the Federation of Yugoslavia.

After the quarrel between Tito and Stalin, Father definitively lost his native fatherland Albania, which identified itself with Stalinism nearly to the brink of self-immolation. Following the ecstasy of victory, the border that had until recently not existed between Albania and Yugoslavia now became one of the most cursed and impassable borders in Europe. In Father's mind, it was fatal that the river flowing from the lake traversed the border of his native land and entered back into Stalinism. He feared that, as Igor had predicted, Stalinism would begin by severing the path of the eels in search of new sources of energy and light for the New Man. Still, he hoped his fate would unfold quietly and auspiciously. Hope also intensified Cvetan Gorski's battle to save the pathway of the eels, in fulfillment of Igor Lozinski's last wish.

After his short but significant friendship with Igor Lozinski, Father continued meeting with Cvetan Gorski, who was leading his own battle during those difficult times to preserve the memory of their friend by opening his museum and keeping his ideas alive. He, too, was not certain whether it was worth fighting during the Stalinist era. It was easy to lose one's life and for the vast collection dedicated to the lake habitat be submerged once again.

Father still awaited some final sign that would tell him whether to leave this town by the lake; he had decided that the outcome of the last battle in Cvetan Gorski's war against those in power over the fate of the path of the eels would be an omen. He also had to consider what the implications would be for Mother, for us children, and the family before reaching a final decision regarding our exit from exile.

Mother remained the eternal seismograph of Father's movements across the Balkan relief of his illusions. She could not keep everything to herself, and bear it alone, but with exceptional sympathy and respect, she listened to Father and let all his doubts flow into her soul and her thoughts; Everything she could take from him and hold onto supported and broadened the significance of all that was unspoken in the silence that existed between them; her soul seemed to flow together with his. There was an unseen thread crossing from one soul to the other. It was their love that made them stronger as they protected the family from the blows of fate.

Chapter 21

Who knows why Little Eel Drimski was called Little Eel — whether it was because when still in diapers, he wriggled about and wanted to move straight away into life, or whether his godfather had a secret he alone possessed. Whatever the reason, Little Eel remained Little Eel; he grew accustomed to his name. And the older he grew, the more the name suited him. From early childhood he managed to slip through all of life's vicissitudes, both large and small; he was as clever as can be; he muddled along and got ahead in life. No one could quite figure out how he managed to muddle through. The name stuck with him permanently.

Little Eel Drimski adroitly maneuvered his way through the Bulgarian and Italian occupations, through the German Fascist period. He eeled his way through Stalinism as well. He remained ever worthy of his name. When the sun of freedom rose over the people living by the lake country, he set himself up pretty well, not exactly in the first rows where the brightest rays shone, but somewhere where he would neither go unnoticed nor appear too prominent. Neither in the sun nor in the shade.

If he wasn't the first, in the front ranks of those battling Fascism, he found himself among the first in the battle for Communism. First he swore by Stalin, but then put his store in those who bravely drove the Russian Leader of the Masses from the people's consciousness. And so, willy-nilly, Little Eel became a hero of the new era.

In this new era of freedom, he considered changing his name. Little Eel? Little Eel, indeed! Who would trust him with such a name! They would doubt his intentions. He would always be suspicious, slippery, indecisive. But Little Eel was well positioned among the new leaders. At other times, he had thought about changing his name, but had kept putting it off. He left the changing of his name for this new era, when he expected to be given power and a high position in the party hierarchy. That old thought came back to torment him: how could he step into the party leadership with the name Little Eel? He must have a heroic name, a name worthy of the new era. He well knew — by who knows which party channels — that he would be asked about his godfather's intentions, about his class background, about why his parents had agreed to the name.

At one point, he had decided to change his name. A number of names circled in his head. First there were the names of heroes, foremost among them Stalin, with all its derivatives. Despite the fact that, at that time, the number of names for the leader had multiplied, even if he were to change it to any one of them, he would still be called Stalin. But in the end, Little Eel kept his own name. Better to remain Little Eel, he thought, than to have someone else's name, someone with a changeable fate. When all was said and done, he was used to his own name, Little Eel, and how could he simply break the habit? Later, when Tito broke with Stalin and when those who had but recently been brothers now became fierce enemies, Little Eel remained quite happy — happy indeed — with his name. He had had to struggle to get used to the name he had been given at birth. Now he had to get others used to it.

In those first years of freedom and under Stalinism, life in the Balkans was what the people deserved. Here life flowed along where the river flowed from the lake; it flowed along with the new times. Little Eel Drimski struggled to swim out of his lake and make it on dry land. At the first meetings held after the war, he railed—oh, how he railed — against domestic enemies and those who had recently been their minions, against the speculators, against the villagers who did not wish to give up their land and enter into voluntary cooperatives, against every privately owned business, against all who did not dance to the new leaders' tune.

After Little Eel Drimski won renown in this town where the river flows from lake for his work, the local leaders, with the consent of those higher up, entrusted him with the historic role of directing not only the people, but the water as well: the lake water, the water of the river, the waters of all the streams that flowed into the river and into the lake. He had been a hero on dry land, not on water.

"Is someone playing a joke on me," Little Eel Drimski said to himself. "Or do they really know that I am all-powerful?"

Little Eel Drimski knew all about the source waters, both big and small. He knew each tiny rivulet flowing into the lake that had anything to do with the people living in its vicinity. He also knew about disputes that took place high in the mountains surrounding the lake, about quarrels between opposing villagers, about who drew more water from the spring for their village or from the river flowing between two villages. He opposed those who wanted more water, who acted as if they were masters of the flowing water. Here he revealed less a sense of justice than a willingness to use force.

And so Little Eel made a name for himself. He even received a medal from the Republic for meritorious service. At first, he wore it every day, pinned to his chest, later only on state holidays or when someone from the upper echelons of government visited the city. The medal emboldened him still more in his actions. He divided the waters, giving some less, others more, as he deemed fit. He had a whip and a revolver; who would say a peep when they were thirsty? There would certainly be water for everyone! See that lake? It's as big as a sea! There would be water for everyone! It was possible to quench the thirst of all the people in the world, Little Eel concluded, and no one dared contradict him.

One morning, Little Eel Drimski was summoned, along with all the local leadership, to a meeting of the municipal party committee, at which a representative of the Central Committee of the Republic, Comrade Sreten Javorov, would be present. On a slip of paper he read the names of other important people in the Republic's government. Who could remember all those names? There was no time to compose himself.

He was uncertain whether he should pin the medal to his chest. He had never before been summoned to such an important meeting. What was it all about? His wife accompanied him to the outer gate with a jug of water in her hands. She performed the custom for good luck: she poured water on Little Eel's path to make his day a happy one.

Chapter 22

So Little Eel Drimski, filled with uncertainty about the day, set out along the river, hoping that his mind would clear before he got to the party meeting. What was there that water couldn't wash clear? It cleared everything, including everyone's mind.

Little Eel Drimski had carefully tucked his medal in his pocket, just in case. He was still debating whether to pin it on his chest. As he went along, he playfully plucked petals from a daisy like a child: I'll wear the medal, I'll wear the medal not.

And so, playing absent-mindedly, he made his way to the meeting of the party. His game with the daisy told him that he should wear the medal, so he did. Had he put it on a bit earlier, though, while walking along the quay on such an ordinary day rather than a holiday, people would have made fun of him. The medal was large, like those often seen in abundance on the chests of Russian generals in the movies made right after the war, films he took delight in.

Little Eel was calculating everything. As he walked along the river, he met many people. Some greeted him; others avoided him. Little Eel Drimski was sunk in thought. With medal on his chest, he entered party headquarters. He climbed the stairs and headed toward the central hall, where Trim Toska, secretary of the municipal party, was expecting him. He entered with the medal in full view, for good or ill.

Inside, it was as if nothing had changed since those distant Ottoman times: when it was a question of power, power over the people, power still kept its mythic aura. To those subject to power and those who thought they wielded it, power came as if on wings of fate from a great distance, from as far away as possible, from God himself. No matter how much time had elapsed since the fall of the Ottoman Empire, when power was in question, this Oriental fatalism could not easily be uprooted.

That is what Little Eel Drimski was thinking to himself, as if he were some Ottoman vali in a Stalinist vilayet, expecting a decree that could punish him or promote him. Every conceivable thought ran through his head.

He felt immobile, lifeless. For the first time in his life he did not feel worthy of his name: the sly Little Eel will not survive long either in water or on dry land. They are pushing the Little Eel mindlessly toward the weir on the river. And there, of course, he would be driven into a corner; he would be trapped in the labyrinth with little chance of saving himself.

Just look at the situation: it was the party secretary of the republic who had summoned him. It was as though there was going to be some big trial, just like those trials were put on during the time of speculators and traitors. What punishment would they give him? God only knows what will happen to me, Little Eel thought, once again slipping into a spiral of doubt and fatalism. He had long ago given up on God; he was among the first to follow the party's atheism.

Not wishing to give any premature sign of weakness, he strode energetically toward the municipal party secretary. He greeted him and then the others he didn't know; he was seeing them for the first time in his life. He greeted them with ease, with a weak handshake, in contrast to his usual custom, for when he was in the mood, he could crush someone's hand in greeting.

As soon as he saw spread out in front of the secretary a large relief map of the lake with all the waters flowing into and out of the lake, his spirits brightened. He looked down and touched his medal. Then a new wave of doubt overtook him. Had he overstepped his powers with the water and the people? Had the villagers complained, and he would now be punished for his actions? He was well acquainted with his offences, all the times he had gone too far and used force.

He calmed down a bit when engineers from the Republic Ministry of Civil Engineering and Urban Affairs as well as local representatives of the government entered the hall. But when he caught sight of Cvetan Gorski, the biologist, among those present, he was rattled and new doubts washed over him. The wily Little Eel struggled to remain calm. Images of Cvetan Gorski and his friend with a suspicious past, that White Russian Igor Lozinski — who knew how he had made his way to their town? — churned in his head.

During the war, Little Eel Drimski had played no role. He had had other priorities. He wondered then how Igor Lozinski's fame had taken root in the souls of all these people. These same people who remained fairly indifferent to governmental orders and appeals of the party. But, he told himself, better not to think about that until he understood what Cvetan Gorski was doing there and who had summoned him.

When the secretary, Trim Toska, a well-known partisan from the area, sensed that there was sufficient quiet for him to impose his authoritative voice, he stood and introduced those present with well-chosen words. First, he introduced all the representatives of the Central Committee of the party, then the representatives of the Ministry of Civil Engineering and Urban Affairs, then the local functionaries, as well as the biologist Cvetan Gorski. Little Eel Drimski expected to hear his own name as well. But it never came. He froze, turned pale, even covered his medal with his hand; he could feel his heart beating rapidly.

Trim Toska noticed Little Eel Drimski's agitation. He wanted to calm him with a gentle look. But that was not sufficient. Trim Toska raised his voice and said, "And now, respected comrades, it is with special pleasure that I present to you Little Eel Drimski, a man of his word and trust, a warrior hardened in the battles with the occupier, but also in the struggles for our reconstruction, a man who has done great service in the liquidation of the class enemy. But his greatest achievement has been his success in introducing order between people and water. No one has done this better than he has, neither in the past nor in the present."

That sly Little Eel Drimski could not believe his ears! He might have expected anything, but not this! He was clearly confused. But he pulled himself together quickly. He stood up, thrusting out his chest to show off his medal. Still, he could not figure out just what was going on. He did not know whether to remain standing or to sit down, whether to wait for Trim Toska to continue speaking or not. Hoping for the best, he remained on his feet. After everyone in the hall had quieted down, Trim Toska continued.

"Dear Comrades," he said, "our great party, in accordance with all local and republic organs of the government, has completed a months-long study of the biographies of our cadres and has decided to entrust the construction of the first hydroelectric station on our river — not far from where the river leaves the lake — to our steeled comrade Little Eel Drimski. The party has decided that Little Eel Drimski will be at the head of the new division for the construction of this hydroelectric station and the regulation of the lake's water."

Now at last Little Eel Drimski collected himself. He calmed down. He stood proudly, eyes focused on the portrait of Stalin with his energetic expression hanging beside the portrait of Tito. For an instant, he even imagined himself among them! But not for long.

"The higher you climb, the more dangerous it gets," he reminded himself. The waves of doubt continued to sweep over him from time to time. This was sticking his head too far into the line of fire! It occurred to him that no one had sought his consent for this new position. But even if they had, no one said no to the party.

Until now, everything had been going well, even though he had heard nothing from either the party or the government about his work. Until this moment, he had been in charge of the fate of people in relationship to water; he was unchallenged in his work. No one had bothered him. He had lived peacefully until now.

Those present, carried away by Trim Toska's lofty rhetoric, did not consider whether Little Eel Drimski had been asked to lead this major construction project; they knew that loyal, trusted cadres were sought for such positions. Listening to Trim Toska's words of praise, the hydraulic engineers had no doubt as to Little Eel Drimski's indisputable political qualifications, even though his professional credentials were still in question. But there was no choice. The party had the last word. And even that clever Little Eel Drimski had enough brains in his head to understand that that they were putting him in charge not for his brains but for his brutality. Though he didn't yet know how much brute force would be needed, and against whom. That was for the party to figure out.

Little Eel remained silent. Although some say that silence is golden, sometimes that is not the case — and who could say whether it was golden at that moment? So Little Eel Drimski did not say a word. He remained standing. Secretary Toska gave him a signal to be seated. Little Eel waited briefly for the secretary to sit so he could remain the last standing, then he adjusted his medal and sat down. He couldn't decide whether he should say something. Should he thank him? But it wasn't up to him to determine when to speak. That was for Trim Toska, who was running the meeting, to decide.

"And now," the secretary declaimed once there was complete silence, "I turn the floor over to Comrade Sreten Javorov, who will greet the assembly."

The representative of the Central Committee, accompanied by wild applause, approached the microphone, adjusted it, and began.

"Comrades," he said, "we are stepping forward into Communism with much more powerful and more rapid steps than even our most notable strategists of Social Communism could have at one time predicted. I must tell you this at the outset. The fiery march of liberation and the glory of our Stalin must continue through the vitality of the working class in the construction of our country.

"The major planners of development, at the republic and federal levels, from the entire Fraternal Union of Socialist States, have helped us turn each part of our country into a paradise. Heaven on earth exists where it is deserved. By mutual decision, all our advanced Socialist forces, led by our party, have determined that paradise will be established right here in these marvelous domains, beside these sources of water and light. Our scientists and celebrated specialists, with the assistance of experts from fraternal Socialist countries, have noted that in these waters are hidden billions of kilowatt-hours of electric energy.

"We will tame the waters of the lake and those surrounding it, including this pristine river; we will plant a garland of hydroelectric stations. No one in the past ever considered this. Now we will turn these brisk flowing waters into light. Our scientists have discovered the formula for pouring light down from all sides into our heavenly garden of Communism.

"To conclude, comrades, in the name of the Central Committee of the party, I wish you great successes in the realization of this historic task. And to you, Comrade Little Eel Drimski, I wish you success as head of the division in your work for the good of our great party and our people."

There was resounding applause. Everyone stood up, including Little Eel Drimski. At first, he did not know whether he should join in the applause; he didn't want the others to think he was applauding for himself. So he remained silent.

Finally, Secretary Toska concluded the ceremonial part of the meeting and announced the working part for the afternoon, where plans would be exhibited for the construction of the first hydroelectric station at the point where the river flowed from the lake. The experts would speak about their role, but the politicians would not stay silent.

Little Eel Drimski beamed with joy. This was the luckiest, yet most uncertain, day of his life. His medal shone, pinned just above his heart. One could detect the beating of his heart by the medal's occasional rise and fall.

Chapter 23

Little Eel Drimski felt reborn. His mood was celebratory. He immediately took the initiative and organized a lake excursion on one of the larger patrol boats of the lake fleet for Secretary Toska and the representatives of the government and the National Front.

As the boat quickly churned through the water, trailing a large wake, new waves of pleasure filled Little Eel Drimski; it was as though he were soaring through the sky. For a moment, he felt more powerful than all the local leaders, almost up there with the republic secretary responsible for the economic development of the country. But he didn't carry that thought further, a bit afraid that he would go too far.

Little Eel felt most powerful on the lake. On dry land, he was calmer, though there, too, he was as bold as he dared; he held his ground. As he took the helm of the patrol boat, he told himself to remain calm, and steered it toward the monastery that stood at the border between Albania and Yugoslavia.

At that time, the border between these two "fraternal countries" — connected by the bridge of Stalinism — was not guarded as it was in other eras. In the distance, large white, well-anchored buoys marked the border, but those had been placed there just in case, so one could get one's bearings. Here and there, a gull landed atop the buoys, resting in its flight between the two countries.

Soon it was possible to discern the contours of the monastery rising on a high cliff. The patrol boat pulled into the harbor beside the rapid spring waters flowing into the lake. The bubbling of those waters was the only sound that broke the landscape's quiet. Before the spring waters gathered force and flowed into the lake, they created small ponds, heavenly pools in which all the beauty of this incomparable nature was distilled. The waters were crystalline, and not very deep; they revealed the plant kingdom of the lake in streams of striking colors, dominated by shades of blue and green. White swans sailed regally along the lakeshore.

A table had been set beside the nearest pond and the smell of ceremoniously grilled trout filled the air. As the small procession neared the table, the strains of a song resounded. First a revolutionary song, followed by a well-known folk-song. Beautiful young women dressed in traditional costumes resplendent with a mosaic of colors, holding round loaves of bread and salt, waited on the shore to welcome the guests.

"Well! This is one powerful Little Eel," Secretary Toska muttered to himself. "How had he managed to organize this feast? Impressive — good for him," the secretary added under his breath as he observed the blissful and relaxed expression on the face of the republic party secretary.

Aside from the merits he had earned in battle against Fascism and traitors to the country after the war, Trim Toska had also been given responsibility for the "brotherhood and unity of the nations" who lived here in the lake regions. He was not without ambition, and taking advantage of the opportunity for members of ethnic minorities to rise within the hierarchy, he saw he could advance to a higher position within the Republic's government, just at the time when his children would be getting ready for advanced study. But everything depended on how work progressed on the first hydroelectric station and dam.

While the guests greedily gobbled the trout, they discussed plans for the future, the lake always foremost in mind. They all shared the same ambition: to maintain power over the people who lived by the lake, starting with the local functionaries on up to officials at the republic and federal levels. When the functionaries' enthusiasm was at its peak, the girls' song burst forth. It was all so blissful that none of them sensed time's passage.

Little Eel Drimski took charge. He consulted with Secretary Toska and then turned to the republic secretary to ask permission for the working session to be postponed until the following day. The secretary immediately consented. Little Eel set off boldly to the dial telephone carried by the person in charge of security and communicated to those in town of the meeting's postponement until the following day.

When the small "drunken boat" made its way back toward the town where the river flowed from the lake many hours later, it was night, the low-hanging stars had begun to disperse their light across the lake, and the boat carried all its happy passengers as if victors in some joyous battle, of which there were many during those times.

In his new position of responsibility, even though he did not entirely grasp what it involved, Little Eel Drimski had worn himself out running about to ensure that everything was as pleasant as possible for his guests from the Republic. Finally, exhausted but overjoyed, he set off homeward, whistling a lively revolutionary song as he walked along the riverbank, the tune rising and falling with his steps.

The river, alive and calm, continued to flow as it had since time immemorial. Little Eel was alone that night under the low-hanging stars. He was a bit tipsy. All his depression, his defensiveness, all the morning's uncertainty leading up to the announcement of his new position, only now were pushed aside by unrestrained joy and ecstasy. He was alone with the river. He watched as it calmly flowed past; it seemed to challenge him.

He stopped at the spring and shouted loudly: "You wretched thing, you're next! It's between you and me now! I'll show you where and when to flow. We'll pave your banks. We'll give you new jobs to do! You'll turn those turbines, by God! You'll make the lights shine! You'll see what Little Eel Drimski is made of! You'll never be the same after this!"

He gathered his strength and his thoughts and then, having assured himself that he was alone, he launched new threats against the river.

"There is no salvation for you and your eels," he shouted. "As if they could go sailing back and forth in capitalist seas! Childish fairytales! Even if it's true that they come back — the eels' offspring, that is — well now, they'd be capitalist eels, now wouldn't they. They'd be contaminated."

The water continued to flow as calmly as it had through the ages. A bird in flight took Little Eel's thoughts in a new direction. He still needed to get that Cvetan Gorski out of his mind.

"What was that miserable microbe looking to get from the government and the party?" he thought. "He could spread all kinds of infectious diseases. I mean, we forgave him for all those bugs, but he seems to have some still in his head. Then there were all those butterflies that he wasted all our pins on, and then we forgave him for all his concern for the lake sponges — yeah, so they're millions of years old. It's all nonsense that they could be so old!

"They up and made a museum of all that stuff. A stick, that's what we need! That guy will contaminate the lake with the White Guard ideas of that dead Russian scientist. God rest his soul for all the good he did, but what was he looking for, hanging around with that Albanian immigrant? They're suspicious elements! They would've spread some conspiracy! Sure, everyone said they were good people, but how could such sly ones be good? Whatever — the party really has to keep them in their sights. Right now, really right now, they've got no role to play in lake business and the construction of the hydroelectric station."

Little Eel Drimski walked along to the rhythm of a victory march, whistling to quicken his pace as these ideas came to him there by the river and he saw in its waters the eels, those traitors fleeing to the west. With all sorts of thoughts in his head, he reached the front of his house.

There by the door was Mrs. Little Eel waiting for him. The house was all lit up. It was surrounded by darkness. The poor thing had been waiting all day for him; she had been waiting all night, too. Little Eel Drimski had forgotten to send her a message by municipal courier. First of all, to say that everything had ended well, and second, that he had been given a new job. But that is how Little Eel Drimski acted when the party was in question. It came ahead of everything, including his poor wife.

Little Eel Drimski squeezed his wife in a tight embrace and kissed her on the lips. He had never done that out there on the doorstep. Poor Mrs. Little Eel, in tears, did not look at Little Eel but at the windows of the neighbors, fearing that other eyes were watching. Little Eel Drimski scooped Mrs. Little Eel into his arms. He carried her across the threshold as he had but once before — on their wedding night.

Chapter 24

In the morning, as the new day dawned, Little Eel Drimski set off to his office like a new man: refreshed, all dressed up, medal in his pocket. First, he went by the town hall, then to party headquarters, whose buildings were located on both sides of the river. He was first to arrive at the town hall, but Secretary Trim Toska was already at party headquarters. With his permission, Little Eel went to the hotel where his guests were staying. He met them for breakfast. He greeted everyone, then sat down beside Secretary Sreten Javorov, across from the experts from the Ministry for Urban Affairs.

Sipping his coffee, Little Eel entered into lively conversation with Comrade Javorov. Pleased with the discussion, Javorov would pat him from time to time on the shoulder. Little Eel counted the pats. Surely, he thought, they would strengthen his position in the city and would open a pathway for a leadership position at the federal level, even though he felt most powerful when close to the water. Then again, in the capital city of the Republic, there was a river that flowed to the sea, though it was small for his ambitions in comparison with this large watery expanse. He preferred the deep, immovable waters from which a river flowed. Not the other way around. Rapid waters could overwhelm him.

Secretary Toska was at the door of party headquarters to greet the guests and Little Eel Drimski; he led the guests into the great meeting hall. Hanging above the wide desk draped with a green woolen cloth were new slogans: *Together with Stalin into Communism! Waters, Light, Our Future!*
Tito, Stalin, Our Future!
Tables had been placed in a circle. Local representatives of the government, the hydraulic engineers, experts, and various other people were already seated there. Among the last to enter was Cvetan Gorski. When Little Eel noticed him among the last seated, his mood shifted momentarily, and he took Cvetan Gorski's lateness to be a petty provocation. Not even from Trim Toska had Little Eel learned who had invited Cvetan Gorski to the meeting.

Trim Toska was a sincere and open man, one who told the truth directly, but who could also keep silent. At that moment, Little Eel thought to himself that someone from the Republic must be protecting Cvetan Gorski; it wasn't his business to go digging around where he shouldn't. Especially where it concerned water.

The republic secretary responsible for economic questions, Sreten Javorov, occupied the central place; Trim Toska was seated at his right, and Little Eel Drimski on the left. Little Eel had not imagined that he would be given such a position. Had he known ahead of time, he would have put on the medal. Still, from time to time he touched it in the left pocket of his coat. All was quiet in the hall. Everyone had settled down. They were waiting for Sreten Javorov to speak.

It was as if a trial were beginning, a trial of the lake, of the eels, of nature, and, no less, of people, Cvetan Gorski in particular. He felt as if he had been simultaneously charged and sentenced. He also had to serve as lawyer for his fate. Still, the presence of hydraulic engineers, experts, and other professionals gave him hope, a tiny ray of hope, even though he did not believe that they would be on the side of science over politics. Cvetan Gorski regretted that he did not have at his side the eminent scholars devoted to the lake from other parts of the country. He was the only biologist present at the meeting. He also bore the weight of representing the knowledge and mind of Professor Igor Lozinski, founder of the one-and-only "university" for the study of the lake's natural habitat.

In those difficult days of Stalinism, when the newly created working class led by ignorant secretaries of little talent could easily settle accounts with the intellectuals, there was a quiet, discreet, but pervasive solidarity from all sides concerning Igor Lozinski, his work, and the mission given to Cvetan Gorski. Little Eel Drimski knew many of these anonymous supporters, who had, incidentally, rescued the collection of precious samples of lake flora and fauna, in those difficult times when one could lose one's head for a single wrong word. He had them in his sights. If it became necessary ... But he let it go for now. He restrained himself. He knew quite well that no matter how powerful the party and government were, these people were connected by kinship or friendship; they were godparents, in-laws, linked by every sort of relationship. They were tightly bound and did not loosen those bonds easily. Little Eel was well aware of this.

Sreten Javorov began to speak. In his opening remarks, he announced that he would give the floor to the experts, the hydraulic engineers, and finally to Cvetan Gorski. Little Eel expected to hear his name mentioned as well, even though he didn't know what he would say. He felt like talking right then; the urge was stronger than he was. Why, hadn't he been first to talk at all the town meetings? He told himself that it was smarter now to listen, to talk when he was told to, even though that was difficult for him.

Secretary Javorov spoke with a lowered tone, different from that of the day before, less emotional and revolutionary, but direct nonetheless. He, too, had an order to carry out, a directive from higher up, from farther away. He could not accomplish it with the high style or peremptory tone to which he was accustomed. He had to be blunter, more precise in presenting the major points of the plan. There were smart people there, scientists. He himself was an economist by profession, a specialist in planned economies, just what the times demanded.

No matter how clear the directive, he had to balance it with the realities of life. This was not simply some party meeting where one had to give a party address to which people half listened, half didn't, and among those who listened, half understood, half didn't, and in the end resulted in neither good nor evil. Sreten Javorov was clever enough this time not to mix black and white. A calm, rational flow of this project had to prevail. In sum, he wanted to draw as much benefit as possible from the assembled group, to gather a more complete understanding before final acceptance of the project to construct hydroelectric stations and dams on the river. He had to be direct but cordial with these well-known scientists.

The decision to construct hydroelectric stations had been proposed in the most general terms at the highest level of government, but it had to be carried out scientifically and the people had to be brought into line for these new endeavors. In an emphatic tone, Sreten Javorov read his important address.

"Comrades, we are now at the moment of an epochal transformation into the New Man. Since time immemorial no greater endeavor has been undertaken in these regions than the construction of a hydroelectric station. Our task is of historic significance, encompassing numerous disciplines. The strategists of our party have wisely divided the country into regions and then determined where it is both possible and advisable to build. Comrades, industry must develop to elevate society, to raise up our people who still bend over their wooden ploughs. We have come to realize that the lake harbors enormous energy, energy that must be exploited to the last atom for the benefit of the New Man. Our ultimate goal is to correct nature, to make the crooked straight, but in an intelligent way."

Listening to these words, Cvetan Gorski recalled one of Igor Lozinski's favorite sayings: "Man would conquer nature and enrich it only when he knew how to submit to it." He listened attentively as the speech continued.

"The New Man" the secretary was saying, "will be tempered only through the construction of great, significant engineering projects! The entire Earth will be an eternal construction site. We must bear in mind the experience of our Soviet brothers under Stalin's leadership who, through millions of sacrifices, played the decisive role in the victory over Fascism and the liberation of nations. Our Soviet brothers continued that great war in the construction of a new society that is of major significance for all mankind. They have made of their Soviet land, stretching to far-off Siberia, a true paradise! You have but to watch the Soviet film now showing in our theatres, *The Siberian Land*, and you will see!

"However, comrades, remember this: one of the first and most decisive battles that Soviet Man has waged was bound to the intense struggle — the eternal revolution — to extract ever more energy from Mother Earth for the benefit of man, to discover in the earth endless sources of light. The Soviet experience, comrades, is historically instructive for us. Do you know how the great Lenin defined Communism?"

The secretary raised his head from his notes and looked out into the hall. He was not, of course, looking for an answer but rather catching his breath before continuing. At that moment, Little Eel Drimski felt as though he were again at the "Communist ABC course," in that era when courses were first being organized for the illiterate. Little Eel had a quick mind, and everything that would be of use to him stuck with him, especially where questions of water and electrical energy were concerned.

He stood up and said, "Comrade Secretary, I know how Lenin defined Communism."

A wave of muffled laughter spread through the room, which for a second made Little Eel lose his nerve. But he collected himself. He glanced at Secretary Javorov and sensed his approval, and so he continued boldly: "At the

Eighth Party Congress of Soviets in Russia on the 20th of December 1920, Comrade Lenin said that Communism was the union of the Soviets and electrification."

"Well done, well done, Comrade Drimski! That is precisely what the great Lenin said."

A feeling of joy washed over Little Eel. But even at that moment, he could not ignore Cvetan Gorski's look. He wanted to say something else, but he composed himself. It was Secretary Javorov's turn.

"According to the great Lenin," the secretary continued, "there was no true development without electricity. Light and light alone would enlighten even the darkest souls. However, for the sake of truth, one must acknowledge that the task of turning the great Lenin's dream into reality fell to Stalin. Thanks to the path set by Lenin and realized by Stalin, during the period between 1928 and 1932, that is, during the first five-year plan, the production of electrical energy was increased fivefold, through exploitation of hydroelectric resources."

As he listened, Cvetan Gorski recalled the suffering Igor Lozinski and his generation endured when, during that same period, in search of those new sources of energy, the White Sea Canal was built. At issue was not only the cost of those thousands of lives that paid for the electrical energy, but also the question of its purpose, still largely unrealized.

It was clear to Cvetan Gorski what the secretary was aiming at. He was aiming at the waters of the lake. He was heading to the decision Igor Lozinski had warned them about on their last night together. Cvetan Gorski wanted to respond immediately. But he held himself in check; he was also constrained by the fixed stare of Little Eel, who observed his every movement, while contemplating that the time had come for him to act as director of construction.

As Cvetan Gorski listened to the secretary, Igor Lozinski's words came to him: "The knowing error is worse than a crime." But everything was directed toward justifying the error in advance, with the result that some were held as hostages, scapegoats, and denounced as political agitators, including those deemed to be specialists. These thoughts came to Cvetan Gorski while he listened to the secretary.

"Comrades," the secretary continued, "the wave of Social-Communistic transformation has reached the shores of our lake as well, with its river that connects us to the sea and to the world. It has been calculated that in all of Europe, we have the largest source of clear, potable water, of which, in the future, there will be less in the world. However, these waters are mute, deaf. We are not aware of the wealth that their currents carry. At night, look at the many mountain villages around the lake. They disappear in the darkness. We must bring these waters to life, draw out their energy, their light, in order to see the New Man more clearly."

From time to time, Secretary Sreten Javorov was carried away by his rhetoric, adding emotional touches to hold and animate the attention of most of those present. Then he changed tone.

"Comrades, " he said, "the projects to be given strategic priority for the rapid development of our republic — in accordance with the possibilities they provide as well as the needs of our federation and the International Socialist Union — have been assessed at the highest level, both at the federal level and in consultation with the Union of Fraternal Socialist Countries. Our republic has a historic opportunity to obtain its own major industrial projects for economic development, particularly in the mining sector, that will exploit our rich deposits of ore and precious minerals. In the capital city, there are plans for construction of a foundry that will employ tens of thousands of people."

"But why not build foundries where the ore is located?" Cvetan Gorski thought, wishing for the first time to contribute to the secretary's thoughts. But he suppressed the desire. He had come for another purpose; his time would come. He continued to listen attentively to Sreten Javorov, a man no one would dream of interrupting.

"As I have stated, " continued the secretary, "it has been decided at the highest levels to execute several projects of wider strategic significance: the construction of two large hydroelectric stations, one near the lake, the other near the border with our western neighbor with whom we are in fraternal Socialist union. It is anticipated that our neighbor will construct hydroelectric stations on those parts of the river within its borders. This will be a true bridge that will further our joint path to Communism. And so, comrades, for the first time in the history of this region, turbines will begin to turn, mammoth turbines, which will bring us closer to developing our own heavy industry.

"You well know that one does not reach Communism with goats and donkeys, nor can oil lamps light the pathway to our future. Comrades, our endeavor is complex, and our people are not accustomed to such tasks. But through this work, particularly the construction of large dams to contain the river and create reservoirs, our people will truly be transformed. Later, we will also build a system of hydroelectric stations, first one, followed rapidly by a second and third. The sources of energy are endless.

"I will not say more concerning the technical aspects of the construction of the dams. Our tempered hydraulic engineers are qualified at the high levels attained by engineers in the Soviet Union and other Socialist countries. Comrades, let us understand one another. The construction of the hydroelectric stations will unfold over an extended period and will require great sacrifice and effort — historic effort.

"During the first phase, it will be necessary to alter the river's course. Then, after the construction has been completed, which could take two to three years, the river must be completely dammed. The construction of the first dam will provide us with tremendous, valuable experience. Our hardened working class — joined by villagers, soldiers, and our young people — will construct the dams.

"The dams, about which our seasoned specialists will speak, will be earthen embankment dams. Great quantities of clay, stone, and gravel will be piled up; then the cement foundations will be constructed, across which a regional highway will be built that will serve as a bridge between the two shores."

"The poor eels, the poor eels," Cvetan Gorski whispered to himself, but his moment to speak had not yet arrived.

The engineers then spoke at length about the construction of the hydroelectric stations; the economists discussed plans concerning construction and the income it could generate. No one, not a single person, has mentioned the eels, thought Cvetan Gorski, as he listened to them. They had probably left that for him.

Secretary Javorov had not, however, forgotten the eels. He indicated that Cvetan Gorski would speak about them as well as the natural habitat of the lake.

"Our party always thinks dialectally, holistically, and with attention to detail," the secretary said. "Of course, we have not forgotten about the migration of our lake eels, which, together with the trout, are the pride of our lake. We remain open to all possible methods of preserving the path of the eels in conjunction with the construction of hydroelectric stations on the river.

"There are proposals for the construction of fish ladders running parallel to the dams, on which the eels would also travel so that they would not be cut off from their migration path. But let us be clear. In regard to this, several things must be considered: the water diverted for the new fish ladders must not reduce the quantity of water entering the hydroelectric station, for doing so would increase the cost of producing electricity. Other plans have been proposed for conserving the path of the eels. Further consultations will be conducted, and the experiences gained from numerous similar projects across the broad Socialist union extending from the lake to distant Siberia will be studied.

"Further, with the increase in the amount of water flowing from the lake, the question of the lake's water level is critical. But our party has a solution to this problem as well. You are well aware of the fact that there are many rivers and streams around the lake. We will reverse their current! It is anticipated that the first to be reversed will be the river closest to town, because it will not require much effort. Projections show that this is certain to raise the level of the lake, on which the effectiveness of the construction of our hydroelectric stations on the river also depends."

Cvetan Gorski reacted immediately: this would be catastrophic for the lake and all its fauna! It would be the end of the lake! He wanted to comment immediately on what Sreten Javorov was saying, but he was not sure how the secretary would respond. Better to wait a bit. After all, changing the course of the nearby river, making it flow into the lake, was the weakest, most objectionable part of the project. It was obvious that with that move, the lake would be sacrificed. He tried, however, to keep his attention on the next phase of Sreten Javorov's presentation.

"I am aware, comrades, that great sacrifices will be sought for the realization of these projects," the secretary continued. "We must sacrifice something from the lake as well, even, if necessary, the path of the eels. For us, the production of electric energy at this phase in the building of our country is our most sacred obligation.

"I nearly forgot to mention that if work to construct parallel ladders for the eels turns out to be too expensive, the party will obligate the state to introduce into law a directive to find means to secure the rejuvenation of the eels by supplying young eels from the waters of fraternal Socialist countries. But let us leave all this for biologist Cvetan Gorski to explain as the first speaker at tomorrow's session. His presentation will be of invaluable significance."

News of Cvetan Gorski's presentation struck Little Eel like a bullet to the heart. He asked himself, as he did whenever he thought of Cvetan Gorski, "Who is going to be the bigger fish: me or him, the offspring of an immigrant? But let it go, time will tell. We will hear what song that chick sings tomorrow. One day, he'll surely fly into my cage!"

At the end, however, Sreten Javorov did indeed turn to Little Eel and gave him the floor. He was a bit flustered and found it difficult to speak. Sreten Javorov immediately spoke for him.

"Respected colleagues," he said, "Comrade Little Eel Drimski, in the name of the leadership, invites all those present to an eel dinner at the Lake House restaurant."

There was a burst of applause. Poor Little Eel did now not know whether to feel glad or insulted. But he let it go. What was most important was that the secretary had spoken for him and that he remained the center of attention. The time would come for him to rise higher. As if by reflex, he turned his gaze again to Cvetan Gorski, and that bolstered his inner confidence.

"Is he going to come to my eel dinner to see for himself those eels, big ones and small ones, roasted on the spit, to see where they really belong?" he asked himself. "If he doesn't show up, it'll be clear whose side he's on, and then he won't be able to ram down our throats his ideas of what we at the head office should do with the eels. Really now, we are not going to change the five-year plan for our country's development on account of those damn little eels, are we?"

Cvetan Gorski had had enough of the obvious farce that Little Eel Drimski had concocted and was now playing to the hilt in the great shadow of the party. But for him, it was still significant whether Little Eel would be lost in the shadows or whether he would emerge from them only to be cast under different shadows. And indeed, that is precisely what Little Eel Drimski himself was afraid of.

Chapter 25

Night had already descended on the lake. There was not a cloud in the sky. Lamps were lighted around the lake, and they sparkled like a necklace of pearls. The very idea of borders, of a lake divided, disappeared. Those who had been present at the meeting were on their way to the Lake House, a restaurant not open to the public.

Some strolled along the river. Cvetan Gorski did not go to the restaurant with the others but chose his own path home. First, he headed toward the spot where the water flowed from the lake; he went up to the water's edge. The day had filled him with anguish. He walked the same path where, several years earlier, he had walked with Father and Igor Lozinski for the last time.

He grew sad. Continuing on, he reached the front of our house. He wanted to stop and enter. But he held back. He looked toward Father's room. He recognized the golden light pouring from the lamp and a sweetness filled his soul. He was gladdened by the thought that here beat the heart of friendship, a heart that beat in solidarity with the great path of the eels, in unison with the vanished soul of their great friend Igor Lozinski, savior of the life in the lake.

Filled with such heavy thoughts, he did not want to burden Father. Still, they had agreed to meet at the conclusion of that historic meeting on which the path of the eels and the future of those who lived in this region depended. He passed by our house and approached the river again. He continued, hurrying along. He turned again to look toward Father's library. The golden lamp could no longer be seen. He imagined Father learning new things, deeply engaged in his study of the uncertain path of the eels as he sought a way out for his family.

Cvetan Gorski hoped that the next morning, when the eel conference was expected to end, he would be able to bring Father good news. Would Father be able to continue along the path of the eels before it was cut off? He could not free his mind from the despair Little Eel's overbearing arrogance had unleashed. At home, he stayed up late into the night, deep in thought regarding the day to come. He must get his thoughts in order. He must find the right words for tomorrow's meeting if he was effectively to oppose Sreten Javorov, Little Eel Drimski, and all the other persecutors of the lake's eels.

Finally, just before dawn, he fell asleep. For the first time since he had vanished from this Earth, Igor Lozinski appeared in his dream: He dreamed that his friend had returned to distant Russia. He spoke of how he had discovered the escape route from the White Sea Canal. That path had to exist! Stalin had recognized his errors. Especially his error in building the White Sea Canal. He had abandoned it due to the disruption it would cause to the path of the eels. Now Russia was open. One could freely leave the country. One could travel freely from city to city, from republic to republic. Igor Lozinski was happy at last in his own country. The eels once again connected all of Russia with Europe and the world.

In this dream, Igor Lozinski encouraged his student Cvetan Gorski to be calm and dignified at tomorrow's meeting. He should not let minor provocations distract his attention from the path of the eels. The path of the eels was, in fact, the path of the people. And even if they committed this error, they would not conquer the eels. The eel would find its path. It was older than mankind.

Igor Lozinski appeared to him much older, with a long, white beard, and near the end of the dream he began to move away toward a cloud hovering above the spot where the river flowed from the lake. Cvetan Gorski wanted to tell him that his collection of lake fauna was holding up well, including the eels on their path. But Igor Lozinski continued to move away, until he vanished in a cloud. Cvetan Gorski called after him. He begged him to stop, to return.

Cvetan Gorski's wife became alarmed and entered the room. Cvetan Gorski awoke, drenched in sweat. He rose and calmed his wife. It was a dream, he said, a dream in which he had seen his departed friend for the first time.

His wife composed herself. This was not the first time in those difficult days when her husband struggled to save the path of the eels that she had found him talking in his sleep. She knew what burden he carried.

While he ate his breakfast the next day, Cvetan Gorski arranged his notes for his presentation at the meeting. He had to discuss openly that critical word "dam," the dam that those planners of the bright future planned to erect on the river, a Balkan wall blocking the eels from their path to the sea.

With a look of concern, his wife watched him as he set off with rapid steps along the river; he did not look at its clear waters that, though flowing in the opposite direction, also seemed to follow him with concern.

He was the first to reach the hall. Trim Toska arrived next. Then Little Eel Drimski, accompanied by Sreten Javorov and all the others. Without introduction, as had been announced, Sreten Javorov gave the floor to Cvetan Gorski. The biologist made his way to the lectern. This time, Little Eel Drimski did not follow him with his persistent gaze. Something seemed to have changed in his demeanor. Had Cvetan Gorski been a member of the party, everything would have been different. They would have been friends. Now, however, Little Eel Drimski was charged with a confidential mission working with the highest levels of regional, republic, and party leadership, while Cvetan Gorski was outside party ranks.

Cvetan Gorski had shown no interest in becoming a member. He had only to say the word, and he would have been in the first ranks, despite his friendship with the Russian immigrant. This thought ran through Little Eel Drimski's mind as Cvetan Gorski authoritatively took his place. As soon as he had his notes in order, he began.

"Respected Secretary Javorov, respected comrades," he said. "I thank you for inviting me to this important meeting concerning the future of our region. As a biologist and student of Doctor Igor Lozinski studying the lake and its ecosystem, I would like to take the liberty to express my views regarding the potential construction of hydroelectric plants and embankments on the river and the raising of the water level of the lake with water from rivers whose currents would be reversed to empty into it. In particular, however, I would like to focus on plans to sever, or modify, the path of the eels."

Little Eel Drimski felt that Cvetan Gorski had begun his presentation in a rather high-handed tone and wondered why he needed to get that Russian immigrant mixed up in these things. When he saw that neither Secretary Javorov nor Trim Toska reacted, he thought that there were things that would never be clear to him. But he decided not to get himself mixed up in things that were the exclusive domain of the party. Although he found Cvetan Gorski's style strange and not completely comprehensible, Little Eel managed to look as if he were giving his full attention as the biologist continued.

"History has not been kind to us in the past," Cvetan Gorski said, "nor has our geography given us many gifts. There are few places in the world where history and geography are in balance forever. Before all else, comrades, we are responsible to the history and the geography of our planet, and after millions of years, we must not be guilty of cutting off the ancient path of the eels that runs from these fresh lake waters out to the seas, to the ocean, and back. This route is of biological significance for the planet. We are responsible to humanity — in scientific terms — to save the earth's macro-ecological equilibrium. The dams planned for construction on the river would also become walls that would distance us from Europe and our allies."

As he listened, Little Eel Drimski signaled his unease by noticeably turning around. First he looked questioningly at Trim Toska, then at Sreten Javorov. But when he noted that the republic secretary was following the speaker with visible interest and nodding his head from time to time, he reconsidered his reaction.

"If they're not taking into account our relations with our allies and Stalin, there's no point in my getting mixed up in it," Little Eel said to himself and again adopted the pose of attentive listener following Cvetan Gorski's talk.

"According to the estimates of paleontologists," said Cvetan Gorski, "the eel first made its appearance more than a hundred million years ago, at the time that dinosaurs walked the Earth."

When he heard that, Little Eel Drimski could no longer contain himself. He whispered to Trim Toska:

"What! Did you hear that? That dimwit is back with the dinosaurs. Just so long as he doesn't lead us there. He can go there himself. He's turning plain old eels into heroes!"

Trim Toska heard what was said, but he did not reply. Though others could not make out what he had said, Little Eel's words had for a moment broken the silence. Secretary Javorov, who had begun taking notes on what Cvetan Gorski was saying, begged for quiet. Emboldened, Cvetan Gorski continued.

"It is rare for any other living creature on this planet to follow the course of human destiny the way the eel has," he said, "and as man, in turn, has followed the fate of the eels. However, respected comrades, for all of us here, it is the European, indeed Balkan, eel — whose fate our party must determine today — that is of special interest."

"That's right, the party will determine it," Little Eel whispered to Trim Toska, "and not you, you butterfly chaser."

Secretary Javorov clearly heard Little Eel's commentary this time but paid no attention to him. The poor guy doesn't understand irony, Little Eel told himself, but the secretary finally had to speak up.

"Comrade Gorski," he said, "we beg you to direct your remarks to the living world of the lake, to questions related to the importance of their survival, particularly in regard to changes in the composition of lake water due to construction of hydroelectric plants and the reversing of the course of the nearby rivers into the lake, as well as to the eels, for which it is anticipated that special measures will be taken. Of course, the party you refer to must have the final say concerning these questions."

"I thank you, Comrade Javorov," Cvetan Gorski continued, "First I wanted to point out the significance of our lake and the preservation of its biological integrity for all humankind. If we succeed in saving the purity of the lake, which is a priceless source of potable water for an entire thirsty continent, then Europe — a continent that will one day surely be integrated and united economically — will have an ever increasing need for this clean, natural oasis. The value of the lake will keep increasing. It will surely be worth more than billions of kilowatts of electrical energy."

Little Eel Drimski saw in these words an open provocation against the project. Now Trim Toska also wanted to stand. He was very upset. In the hall, especially from the back rows, shouts of disapproval rang out. All eyes turned to Sreten Javorov. They all wondered whether this would give the secretary grounds to abandon the project. But to everyone's surprise, Sreten Javorov, an economist, gave a sign to Cvetan Gorski, who had fallen silent, to continue.

"The day will come when the lake will become a sanctuary for our planet," said Cvetan Gorski, encouraged again. "People will come from all corners of the Earth, from east and west, to delight in the well-preserved authentic representatives of worlds long extinct that no longer exist elsewhere on our planet."

This was the era when Stalinism was still at its height. However, the coming decline and fall of that era could be sensed. At that time of the Cold War, when an iron curtain had descended on Europe, imposing an impenetrable border between peoples, Cvetan Gorski knew that there were minds in the country that opposed the new division caused by Stalinism. Yet it was still a time when such "mistaken ideas" as those he was expressing now could easily have led to a term in prison with no return likely. Especially given that he was a loyal student of that sworn anti-Stalinist Igor Lozinski.

But Cvetan Gorski was prepared to sacrifice everything, even his life, when the lake itself was threatened. Paying no attention to any possible reaction from those narrow minds around him and having found, paradoxically, a sort of ally in Secretary Javorov, he continued.

"As you know," he said, "the waters of our lake are deep. But every depth has its bottom. Its limits."

Cvetan Gorski looked only at Sreten Javorov as he spoke. It seemed that in the part of Sreten Javorov's soul that resisted the pervasive ideology of the time there was space in which the brave, clear, logical, and natural thoughts of Cvetan Gorski could find fertile soil.

It was also clear that the courageous biologist was preparing to address the other weak point of the project: the plan for a new river to pour into the lake, the consequences of which, according to the firm assertion of Cvetan Gorski, would lead first to the destruction of the identity and integrity of the lake's flora and fauna, and then, over a long period, to the very disappearance of the lake itself, no matter how deep it was.

Cvetan Gorski explained how several European lakes had disappeared due to river deposits and how other lakes throughout the world had also been threatened over the course of millennia. At that moment, he recalled one of the things Father had said and often repeated in conversations with Igor Lozinski when he spoke about his work on the Balkan empires through a study of their collapse.

"Not a single empire that ruled over the lake raised a hand against its waters despite many plans to change the appearance of the lake," he said. "Not under Roman rule, nor Byzantine, nor during the many centuries of the Ottoman era. Good sense always prevailed. Surely, our party will also refrain from doing this and find the correct path between the imperatives of progress and the eternal laws of nature."

Not even this ambiguous statement, which other members of the party took as an open provocation, drew a reaction from Sreten Javorov. Little Eel

Drimski would have felt like an eel left too long on dry land had he not now interrupted for the first time.

"Comrade Javorov," he said, "biologist Gorski has strayed far off course. He has waded deep into politics. If this continues, I do not know how we will get to construction of hydroelectric plants in accordance with the party directives. Nor do I see the purpose of the role I have been given."

Little Eel would not have been Little Eel had he had not spoken up. But even he had enough brains to sense that Stalinism was not what it had been in the early days after the war. The people were now divided, polarized. Little Eel sensed that even Sreten Javorov appeared to have separated himself from the hard-core Stalinists. He was now convinced that he owed his positions more to those hard-core ideologues who were still strong and less to the secretary who was heading off in Cvetan Gorski's direction, down the path of those damned eels.

After Little Eel Drimski had spoken, a wave of anxiety spread through the hall. It was assumed that Cvetan Gorski would be removed from the podium and ejected from the meeting. As expected, Secretary Javorov was first to speak.

"Comrade Drimski," he said, "calm yourself, relax. The party has before it a historic decision. It must take into consideration all points of view — in particular those expressed by the professional cadres — in order to make the correct decision, to which everyone will then be committed."

Little Eel Drimski did not respond; this only confirmed his suspicion that the party was no longer what it had been when, years before, it did not look to others for its decisions. It was now also clear to Cvetan Gorski that he would be free to present his full argument without interruption, something that, at the beginning of the meeting, he doubted he could accomplish. He turned to the topic he was most anxious to speak about.

"Respected Secretary Javorov, comrades," he continued. "As you are aware, our lake draws its waters exclusively from springs. And it is itself a major source of fresh water, an eternal source. There is no other lake like it on the planet. From the point of view of geology, the lakes on Earth have each a clear and calculable end. The main reason for the disappearance of many lakes is, as we have already mentioned, the silt deposits carried by rivers, which fill the lakes. These deposits eventually take over the lakes and the life within them. Every lake with rivers flowing into it has, in fact, an endpoint that can be determined, determined with precision. But we are fortunate" — for a moment he thought of mentioning God, but changed his mind at the last moment; this was, after all, a meeting of the party — "that a river flows out from the lake. Therefore, comrades, if a river were to flow into the lake, it would be fatal."

"This guy sure twists things, just like an eel," Little Eel Drimski remarked again, though to himself this time. "He won't get to the question the secretary asked him about the eels, and the fish ladders, just so his eels are saved."

It was as if Sreten Javorov had heard him, for he next said to Cvetan Gorski, "But now, respected Gorski, what will happen to the eels and their migration path if the project for construction of hydroelectric plants and embankments is carried out and if the level of the lake is raised when the river is redirected into it? According to your views, will we be able to save the path of the eels under these conditions?"

Cvetan Gorski looked for the first time at his notes.

"Generally speaking," he continued, "the construction of the hydroelectric stations will assuredly mean the end of the path of the eels. However, let us suppose that it would be possible to construct parallel fish ladders. Keep in mind that we are in the Balkans and must work with our topography and our particular destiny. You are right, Comrade Javorov, when you say that construction of fish ladders, or construction of a canal or rivulet to the border, together with construction of the hydroelectric stations will cost more, much more, than the electrical energy produced will be worth. We do not even have any guarantees that our western neighbor will agree to complete construction of the fish ladder from the border to the sea, should hydroelectric stations be constructed on the river there. They are already preparing to construct the station 'Light of the Party.' If the directives they receive are similar and come from the ruling center of the Socialist countries, we can expect a joint action as well."

"Here he is again, poking his nose into things that aren't his business," Little Eel Drimski, continued his internal commentary. "Really, is he building this project or is the party? He's even talking about the very center of the Socialist union! This is not going to end well," thought Little Eel Drimski, continuing to talk to himself.

"Our valued hydraulic engineers," continued Cvetan Gorski, "have proposed the construction of fish ladders as part of the project. They have also presented other possibilities for the eels to find a way out through the steep slopes and valleys that make up our Balkan topography. There would need to be complex solutions, requiring significant financial resources, and a great deal of experience. Such fish ladders have been built beside great rivers with dams and hydroelectric plants in America and in Canada. But we are just coming out of a war. Our Balkan topography is irregular, with changing levels of altitude. The mountains, the land, are not fully stable. All kinds of earth tremors are possible; I am thinking of earthquakes. It is difficult to dig canals. The river has cut its deep path over millions of years."

Judging by the reaction of some of those present, Cvetan Gorski sensed that he had moved away from the theme on which he had been invited to speak in his capacity as a biologist. Although there were rumblings of quiet disagreement in the hall, particularly from the local party leaders, and, of course, the reaction from Little Eel Drimski — sometimes aloud, sometimes to himself — Cvetan Gorski considered it the right moment to express his final observations and remarks, which indicated again that he could not free himself of the spirit of his teacher Igor Lozinski.

"Respected secretary, comrades," he continued, still emboldened by the clear support of Sreten Javorov, "today if we do not find an exit route for the eels as we examine the project for the construction of dams and hydroelectric plants on our river, we will forever block their path, a path that was created at the dawn of life on our planet. If fish ladders are too expensive for us, if cutting openings in the dams with lifts suitable to overcome differences in elevation between the river and the dams is too expensive during these years of reconstruction, then rest assured: when future generations of scientists, hydraulic engineers, and biologists arrive, when they discover other sources of electric energy, they will surely insist that the path of the eels be opened again.

"But if the path is severed and then ten, twenty, or thirty years from now it is restored, whatever the cost, other eels will begin to arrive, if they come at all, eels with a different genetic code, a different memory of their lake. If that is possible, those eels will find themselves in a labyrinth with no exit, just like the people themselves in countries with closed borders. Do not let that happen. Let us not build on what we destroy. We, a poor people who have had so many disruptions in our past, cut off from Europe for centuries, let us not sever this wondrous continuity of life that has taken millions of years to be realized."

Cvetan Gorski finished his presentation. He was certain that he had stirred some doubt in those present. Even in Little Eel Drimski. Whereas the beginning of the meeting had been marked by great enthusiasm for the construction of hydroelectric plants on the river and the belief that it would be realized, now nearly everyone felt the worm of doubt gnawing at them.

Some began to fear for the fate of the lake; they had no desire to see some evil spirit enter the waters, ruled by some anonymous and distant central power that had no sympathy with life by this river and lake. Nor did they want to force the eels to flee, along with the trout and all the other life belonging to the lake and its vicinity. Others were concerned about the jobs that the construction of the hydroelectric stations could have brought them.

But Little Eel, poor thing, did not stop cursing the eels — cursing thereby his own name — as he considered the possible twist of fate that hung in the air following Cvetan Gorski's speech. His fears about the biologist seemed to be coming true.

From the outset, Sreten Javorov had a speech prepared to conclude the meeting. It was a speech filled with emotion, similar to the one he had made at the opening of the session. At the conclusion, he was to have announced the immediate start of the project. That is why Little Eel Drimski had already been named director, of course. But the secretary changed his mind. Something had broken; a profound change had occurred in Sreten Javorov. Something had opened. Within him, the dam that was to be raised above the river had collapsed, and the eels now moved freely on their path.

Chapter 26

It was night. The longest night of Father's life. His soul was a compass whose arrow never stopped spinning. It pointed to all corners of the world simultaneously. He was obsessed with the thought of departure. Late into the night, he listened to his peacock-shaped radio, its feathers in a fan — the radio he had carried from Istanbul, across the border, across the lake. For us, the radio was like a living member of the family. While everyone else slept, Father listened to it deep into the night, its volume low.

This night, as he waited for Cvetan Gorski to arrive from the meeting at which the fate of the eels and their path was to be decided, he listened to the radio, and he could not believe his ears. Tito was preparing to state his historic "no" to Stalin, but he was still not bold enough to state it aloud. Instead he pretended not to hear Stalin's plans to gather the Balkan states around him, thus creating a federation he could later more easily subjugate and rule. If Stalin were angered, Father thought, he might permanently block the borders, and there would be no exit from the Balkans.

And so, Father found himself caught in the rapidly moving current of fate. He circled the room. From time to time, he would spin the globe, unconsciously wishing that it would point out the next stage in his exile. He drew nearer to his books. He began to select those he had taken with him during all the family's migrations.

Mother sensed tension in the house. She had a constant fear that the eels would wriggle themselves deeply into Father's life and the life of the family. That would not be good! But still, at decisive moments in their fate, she left the decision to him. Watching him as he walked among the books and the globe, she began to believe that the books concealed the true exit, just as Father had so often tried to convince her. The right book, the right page or last line, or between the lines, they appeared to hide some secret that Father, with his friends Igor Lozinski and Cvetan Gorski, had sought to discover.

Life had shown her that each book in Father's library had its own fate, a fate still incomplete. And in fact, when one turned the pages of a book, one was turning the pages of its fate. Reading a book meant to bring it to life, to let it live through its destiny. And that destiny might halt at a certain point: a sentence unfinished, an incomplete word. For mother, each book had its soul. But Father believed that his books hid a veritable drama, whose denouement was understood according to the order in which the books were read.

Mother always found some occasion to enter his library. Sometimes, she went in to bring Father a small cup of Turkish coffee, or tea, and often she went in to clear the dust from books that she had already removed several times before, so in the end there was barely a speck left on them. She would look at the books, and it was always the same books lying open, as if the eels had escaped from them and were looking for an exit, seeking their own path. Mother, one could imagine, did not understand any of it.

It was not the first time Father had shut himself in his library, but he had never before paced so from one side of the room to the other. To her, this was a sign that her husband was facing a critical decision.

"May God keep from him thinking we should flee yet again, now that we have settled so nicely here by the lake," Mother whispered to herself. It was not the moment to relocate. It was not the time. After all, the borders were open, so why was there any reason to flee?

Once again, Father wanted to talk with Mother about his new discoveries about the eels, about their long journey and heroic return. He wanted to pass on to her what he knew of the mythic roots of the lake, the underwater kingdom where an eternal peace and harmony reigned, a blue expanse of goodness and multicolored beauty. But there was no time. All this was so near, in the depths of the lake, yet so distant, unreachable. And Father sensed that Mother lacked the strength to let herself follow his fleeting ideas. Her concern was the cry of the children and the worries that came with each new day. Setting out on Father's search along the path of the eels was not for her.

Mother always wanted to stay put and persevere beside the clear blue waters of the lake, but Father wished to follow the water's current, and now the path of the eels as well. His contemplation of departure always contained an ultimate goal: *return* to the land beside our lake, where we had left our house, fields, vineyards, the watermill on the small river that had for ages flowed into the lake. Father was convinced that *our return* had to be realized in every variation by way of America. The first station on our family's return to its native land had been realized near the waters of the Ionian Sea. From there, he now recalled, his ancestors had moved to the lake.

Was this not the vicious circle of exile he was trying to resolve? Through all kinds of alchemy he sought a way for the family to return. The path of the eels reinforced this belief. This was why he was so opposed to the path being blocked.

With these persistent thoughts in mind, Father waited at home with Mother for Cvetan Gorski — the good angel of his fate — to arrive and give him the fateful news of whether it was time to leave. Should he follow the path of the eels before it was severed, or should he remain in this small town by the river that flows from the lake? Would Igor Lozinski's prediction come true: that is, must the people, the river, and the eels suffer if Stalinism reached the lake, or would there be some way to escape that fate? Anything Cvetan Gorski had to say would play a critical role in Father's plan to continue along the path of his exile, having left his native home, in the hope that one day he would return there himself, or through his descendants.

Cvetan Gorski, meanwhile, had said goodbye to Secretary Javorov, feeling his firm handshake, and set off along the river toward our house. For the first time during these dark days when the path of the eels was being decided he was happy, truly happy. He stepped to the very edge of dry land, right to the bank of the river. He wanted to spread all his happiness to the waters and to the eels. He wanted to calm them, to give them courage on their long journey. Father's room was illuminated, one of the few to be lit up at nighttime. Mother opened the gate for Cvetan Gorski. She sensed the joy on his face.

Father was waiting for him with impatience. He greeted his friend warmly and invited him to sit down in his usual place. Between them was the empty chair that had belonged to Igor Lozinski. It was their first meeting in the house since the departure of their great friend. Father, with visible impatience, asked him right away, "What news are you bringing us, Cvetan, will the dam be built on the river?"

Mother entered at that moment, as if by chance, but she was clearly concerned about Cvetan Gorski's answer. After all, wasn't the decision for the family to leave or to stay dependent on this? She set the coffee down in front of them together with glasses of water, then silently went out. Cvetan

Gorski sipped his coffee, took a sip of water, then, sensing Father's impatience, he began.

"So, my dear friend, when they began to speak, it was enough to frighten you," he said. "They had reached the firm decision to begin construction right away on the first dam not far from the place where the river flows from the lake. But, as time went on, something shifted, something broke in the republic party secretary, who bore the final decision. At the beginning, he spoke with feeling as if he were appealing to the construction workers in attendance. They had even appointed a director of construction. Just imagine, it's that Little Eel Drimski. But when I began my speech, he followed me attentively, and as time passed, it showed little by little in his face and in his eyes that he grasped my thesis that they should refrain, at least for now, from constructing dams on the river, so that the eels might freely follow their path to the sea, to the ocean, and back. I don't understand whether that change came about as a result of something I said or whether it was something else."

Father listened attentively to him and visibly relaxed.

"The secretary, it appears, is an intelligent person," he said. "It is likely that he understood your arguments and drew the correct conclusion."

"I agree. The secretary did appear to be intelligent. However, there must be something else. There has to be! One does not change one's views so easily, even more so when that person is director of the party. Surely, something else is going on."

Father was engrossed in what his friend was telling him.

"Things with Stalin are no longer what they have been," he said. "Affairs at the top are becoming murky. Tito isn't going to do things just to make Stalin happy. Things could explode. There could be war. It has not been widely published yet, but Tito has said no to Stalin."

Quiet descended. They turned their gaze to the empty chair where Igor Lozinski used to sit. They were certain that his spirit was with them. His predictions had begun to materialize. Stalinism had spread to the lake region like an all-consuming plague. It had spread everywhere, on all sides. It enveloped the people, the waters, and all that lived within and beside them. The contagion was spreading along with its revolutionary songs, with unbelievable songs and slogans: man must change to change history, to catch up to the West.

It was unbelievable. Stalinism had erected a border between two fraternal Socialist countries on opposite shores of the lake, and now it was strengthening that border, making it the most impassable in Europe. Fate willed Stalinism to take root in Father's native country but to be uprooted from the country in which we now lived. Although these events had not yet been realized, Father, with the keen intuition of one who had himself been uprooted, sensed it. He wanted to stay ahead of events, to find a way out. He had played hide-and-seek many times with Balkan history. Now he had the Balkan eel to lead the way.

His decision had ripened within him. It was time to leave. He had only to convince Mother. He hoped he'd succeed, as he always had before. In Father's mind, it was clear that he would not be able to follow the path of the eels westward along the river, toward the border of his native land and exit to the sea. There, Father predicted, the border would surely close. There was another route, one that followed the course of a different, longer river that flowed south to the sea.

He decided to follow that route. That is what Father was thinking as he listened to Cvetan Gorski speak about the deferral of the decision to build a hydroelectric plant that would cut off the path of the eels. Father saw a ray of hope that illuminated a possible exit route before the path would be closed completely, first closing off the eels, then, later, the people.

Silence fell over them. Mother was close by, her ear pressed to the wall. She knew that a decision had been reached even before Cvetan Gorski's arrival. She entered the room again, just to see whether they needed anything. But her gaze lighted upon the books Father had set to the side. She understood that those books were to be carried on the impending family migration. That is how it had always been with her family and with Father's books.

Knowing of Father's deep interest in the history of the Balkans through the collapse of its empires, Cvetan Gorski expected Father to speak about the nature of Stalinism and his impression of the new situation. Despite its short duration, the empire of Stalinism had already penetrated deeply into the minds of the people. Sensing Gorski's curiosity, Father began to speak.

"It will be difficult to eradicate Stalinism once it has spread to the people, the lake, the lake region, and the river. Stalinism will take root. It will embolden those who hold the reigns of power, and they will not loosen their grip easily, while those who are subjugated will continue to be oppressed, only more so."

As he listened, Cvetan Gorski felt that Father was bringing to life Igor Lozinski's views on Stalinism.

"The people, my dear Gorski," Father continued, "will be freed from Stalin and Stalinism; he cannot live forever. But it will be difficult for them to free themselves of the Stalinism within them. People here are quiet, calm, docile, accustomed to being conquered. Stalin will surely leave many descendants."

Cvetan Gorski expected Father to expound on the future of Stalinism, which would determine the fate of the construction of a dam on the river. Father, meanwhile, was waiting to learn what would happen to the eels if the hydroelectric stations were to be built after all. There was a kind of symbiosis in their future courses of action where the path of the eels and the fate of the lake were in question.

New trials awaited Cvetan Gorski. He would have to preserve the museum collection that Igor Lozinski had created to display the living world of the lake, and he would have to dream up a plan to withstand new pressures that would surely be applied by the hardcore Stalinists, led by Little Eel Drimski, who sought the construction of the dam at any price.

They spoke long into the night. Both of them felt at a crossroads in the new Balkan labyrinth. They would have to lose themselves in that labyrinth while maintaining hope that an exit would be found. They must follow the path of the eels.

After Mother and Father accompanied Cvetan Gorski to the door and they had said their warm farewells, Father looked at Mother directly in her eyes. He poured into her eyes his kind entreaty; he warmly embraced her and whispered quietly, "We are going."

Chapter 27

We left the town where the river flows from the lake and traveled on the railroad on one of its last trips after the war. The little train traveled along narrow-gauge rails. Surely, this was the last such relic in the Balkans. Some time after our last train trip, weeds overtook the rail line, and the little train vanished into oblivion. That poor little thing: though it traveled along narrow-gauge rails up and down the steep slopes of the Balkan landscape, it would always faithfully make its way to the lake. There was a time when one could follow the rails to our homeland and then continue on to the sea. But now the border between the two countries was also a border between two souls; it kept them from drawing near each other, a border that stopped even that little train.

The trip lasted a long time, too long. The little train was small and old; it had its limitations, and it puffed its way with difficulty up the hills. For us, the train was not gone from the lake forever; this trip would live on in our dreams for years to come, always new, always different. The little train traveled along the river, following the path of the eels, then veered toward the capital city, toward the large river where we would now settle. Father saw an exit there, too, in the river current that flowed south to the sea.

We had brought all we could carry, everything our arms could hold. Most important, of course, were Father's books. Mother also carried the ring of keys, the keys to our *return*, the keys to all our futile dreams and hopes. We arrived at our new house beside the great river, guided by the light of our faithful star.

Mother, to Father's amazement, opened the door of our new home with one of the keys on the key ring, a key to a house by the sea long ago abandoned and forgotten. Father asked himself how Mother always had the right key. We began to carve out our new destiny. Our life flowed on with the great river. The days passed.

One morning at dawn, Father went up to the overhanging balcony that perched above the river. Whenever he felt things were difficult for him amidst his books and he could not find the desired way out, he would go out on the balcony and seek out the river that served as a marker of his fate. The breath of the river rose up to the balcony; when he inhaled, his thoughts were set in motion. It drew him closer to a solution that the books had pulled him from.

He took pleasure in watching the rapid rolling river. His thoughts were carried at once to its two endpoints. It began on the slopes of the nearby mountain, whose summits were nearly always covered in snow. He thought of how the fortunate river crossed the border and spilled into the nearby sea. The river cut across the southern border that had been drawn as a true Balkan wall following two world wars and several civil wars.

He had navigated his own fate in exile along the currents of this river. Yet once again, he confirmed in his subconscious that, just as one cannot step in the same river twice, so, too, was his return impossible. In his thoughts, he imagined every possible means to find an exit from this time imprisoned behind closed borders. He watched the occasional gulls skim the water on their arrival after a daring flight up the river from the sea, and they always seemed to him late-arriving Balkan albatrosses, like those he had rejoiced in as a child, enthralled by the shimmering blueness of their flight.

"The gulls fly right over the border," he repeated to himself, being careful not to speak too loudly, lest someone in the family hear him. Those happy white creatures, flitting points in the blue eternity, fly across the border, guided by their instinctual hope that there was an exit from even the most sealed-off places of human habitation and from their mistaken ideologies.

Following the intuition that never abandoned him, Father attempted to apply another, deeper, meaning to this ordinary natural phenomenon: he imagined in the flight of the gulls as they skimmed long distances above the waterways the possibility that human beings might reach other people in other lands.

While contemplating the path of the eels and thinking of the instinctive migration of birds, Father tried to get at the truth about the migration of peoples, nations, and his own family. Were he to share these thoughts with Mother, their conversation would surely turn to heavenly gateways leading to the divine. For Father, the gulls were here, like the eels in the lake, to bear witness to the fact that there was a way out; but for Mother, their flight, like that of the eels on their path, followed God's command.

Mother would speak quietly to herself, often in silence, then she would give herself over to her many worries, to the demands of us children. She knew, and in the course of her life she had had many opportunities to confirm the fact, that Father would disappear into his library and return with unusual discoveries only when he was again overcome with thoughts of moving. But now times were not as they were during the war, when borders were changing. Now the Balkan borders were closed and leaving was perhaps even more difficult than during the war. There was no way out.

The white gulls moved through the white sky above the great river. Some flew toward the nearby fortress on the hill on the opposite shore, while others continued toward the wooden bridge, toward the neoclassical building of the theater, built in the period between the two world wars. With its outdated baroque style, its statues, and masks, it introduced a European air that contrasted with the neighboring buildings from Ottoman times.

Father stared in the direction of the wooden bridge. Was he imagining things after too much reading and thinking? Standing here next to Mother, he did not want to say it aloud, but he was almost positive that he saw our family friend Guri Poradeci, who years ago, at the beginning of our life as immigrants, had carried us in the old family boat from one shore of the lake to the other. That could only be him! Our old family friend Guri Poradeci, who had successfully escorted us into exile.

Father and Mother's eyes met. They spoke to each other through their silence. It couldn't be anyone else; their looks confirmed that it must be our family friend. Here was the first person from our family circle to cross the border since it had closed.

Mother wondered what this could mean. As if in response, Father whispered, "Surely, new times are coming."

Chapter 28

One of the unfinished journeys in our eternal migrations — one that was so significant for us — played out in a number of different ways in our dreams, through the labyrinths of our subconscious.

What had happened during that fateful night of our departure? What had happened to our ancient family boat, that Noah's ark of our hopes? What had happened to our close friend Guri Poradeci, who was now at our doorstep? Could he simply be an illusion after we had for so long imagined and anticipated seeing someone from our former home? What had happened to all those close to us since our abrupt departure across the lake?

We knew that after Stalin's peace, Stalin's hell had been established in our homeland, at the time when in our new country Tito refused to submit to Stalin but turned instead toward the West. In our childish heads, history was simple; it ended as in fairy tales in a battle between forces of good and evil, usually portrayed as gentle animals against bloodthirsty ones. But now our old family friend was coming to tell us in person what had happened to those close to us and to our country since we had left.

"Is that you, my dear friend Guri, or do my eyes deceive me?" cried Father.

"Yes it is, my friend. Who else could it be? I, too, didn't believe that someday I would come and see you alive and well after the stormy night you left," our family friend said.

In a moment, we were all standing in front of the house. The entryway sprang to life. Something was happening that no one could have predicted. Standing there in the doorway, each of us children had many questions to ask Father's close friend, questions that we had long ago prepared, dreamt up, mulled over in our thoughts and in our dreams. Father's best friend was calm, just as he had been that night when he fatefully guided the rudder of the family boat at the outset of our exile. We all held his arm. For reasons we ourselves could not express, we hugged him as though he were our savior.

"Let our friend come into the house! There will be time enough to answer all your questions," Mother interrupted.

"That's right," our guest said. "I will have time for all of you."

Guri Poradeci was carrying a small suitcase and a small canister, the kind with twine wrapping that could be seen on both sides of the lake. Mother took the container, and it gave forth that familiar scent, the breath of our lake, the only fatherland that survived in our memory.

"To the wife," he addressed Mother as he had in old times, "I have brought you trout and eel from the lake. Everyone in our hometown still remembers your mastery in preparing them."

Mother gave an almost imperceptible smile. She was unaccustomed to compliments. But the moment our friend mentioned eel, she seemed to freeze. Silently, she sought Father's gaze. One could read unease in his eyes as well. What could be the meaning of this eel now? Who was sending it? Was it someone who had heard rumors that Father was searching along the path of the eels to find some way back to his homeland?

Mother was quick to dream up all kinds of ideas about the presence of this eel in our house. We children had our own concerns. All sorts of ideas jostled around in our heads. Whenever we asked for a book from Father's library, the eels stared at us from the opened pages. And now to Father's eyes, this eel, brought from the lake, pulled from the shoals of our exile, could not help but radiate its mythic glory and storied genealogy.

Mother took the trout and the eel to the kitchen; we children went off to school. We were setting off at the last possible moment. Oh, how we wanted to stay with Father's friend, who had brought, along with the eel and the trout, our lost history, our lost time from the other shore. Father and Guri Poradeci headed to the balcony. They sat down on the *minder* by the big window, from where they could look down on the wide current of the river, the fortress on the hill. They stayed there by themselves until late at night.

We children were already in bed by then. Our dreams did not circle out to the balcony where Father and Guri Poradeci were deep in thought, glancing from time to time down at the river. We fell quickly into dreams that swelled and swept along like the rapid waters of the river.

With her last strength, Mother finished her last tasks of the day, which awaited her alone, and then she fell into a light sleep, her dreams tempered by the content of the conversation Father and his close friend were having out on the balcony.

They kept glancing at the river, as though they were entrusting to it the thoughts that they hoped would lead them toward a possible exit. It was apparent to Father that his friend shouldered a great secret that was growing bigger, a problem for which he could find no solution. Guri Poradeci had risked his life in crossing the border just to see Father and to share with him what was tormenting him.

After glancing suspiciously to all sides, he fixed his gaze on the flowing river.

"There is something that is weighing very heavily on me, my friend, enough worry for a lifetime," he started. "But let me begin at the beginning. When you left our large family, we were like a body without a mind. You were our only educated lawyer, with a diploma from Istanbul no less, and you were a bright spot in our troubles; everyone thought so, Christians and Muslims. Even in those difficult times, everyone, our family and others close to us, spoke only of your goodness."

Father wanted to interrupt these compliments. He never accepted nor gave them. But his friend continued.

"You truly demonstrated your intelligence to everyone, to our whole clan and all our acquaintances, when you suddenly up and left; but for me, it wasn't a surprise. I helped you row in the family boat to the opposite shore on that fateful night. You left when it didn't seem the time to flee. I don't know how it occurred to you, but you made up your mind to leave."

"That is how it was, my friend," Father said at last, not so much to interrupt him as to give his friend the courage to continue.

"You left, but you condemned yourself to *no return*. And even if you had returned, what good would it have done you, other than that your departure would have been judged less harshly? Some were saying, 'How could they just uproot themselves like that? How could they just leave their land, house, property, so many close relatives?' Many said, 'What strange people, they don't value what they have.' Other harsh words were spoken, but we were the ones cursed, the ones who stayed behind."

Father was silent. He waited for his friend to get to what was tormenting him.

"As time went on, first came the cursed Stalinist period, followed by the cursed era of ties to China. We were cursed, each of us pitted against the other. We came to understand better and better your wise intuition. It was courageous of you to leave. At that time, I was the last one to try to get you to change your mind. I spoke my mind. But you had mind enough for everyone. What a cursed time we live in! We will never get it fully sorted out."

While Father listened to his good friend, in his mind, he saw the war years, the Balkan wars, the world wars, the path to save his family, the path he continued to seek. He did not fully understood what his friend hoped to tell him after this long introduction. Guri Poradeci fell into thought for a moment, sipped his rakija, nibbled the meze, and looked toward the river.

"It seems, my friend, that we are destined to flee," he continued. "Cursed Balkan fate! We are destined by history to flee, and history presses us on all sides."

With these words, Father encouraged Guri Poradeci to open up still more, to forget his pain and to surrender to the great suffering they shared. Father let his friend unburden his soul so that he could reveal whatever truth was bearing down on him.

"A new era arrived accompanied by drumbeats and assemblies," his friend continued. "It was a terrible time. 'You aren't baptized yet? Change your faith. You haven't finished your prayers? Pray to something else! Change again a third time, turn to faith in the party. It will last you through the ages.' It was all trickery. What belonged to others would be taken by force, there would be wine to drink from the vineyards of others, there would be drunkenness. A new justice would be meted out.

"But everything stayed the same. Just the same. Simply more cursed than before. They mixed us up in collectives; we did not even see our own family. What is more, my brother, many were killed. Innocent people. And still many more would be sacrificed, they electrified the borders. Others were imprisoned in their very selves. We do not know what is still to come. Woe to us and to our children."

Father's friend fell silent. He could no longer speak. Several tears ran down his face. The quiet weighed on the two of them with the force of that powerful conversation in the deep Balkan night. From time to time, one could hear the breathing of the children and of the river. Guri Poradeci had still not begun to reveal the most important thing he wanted to tell Father. He could not calm himself easily. Telling these things called forth the sad memory of his suffering.

"We were fortunate, my dear friend," he at last continued, "that even during this terrible fate, we managed to save what of our family could be saved. But there is still much to be saved. Our children, our descendants."

"My friend, what is bothering you now? Tell me. Let us leave aside past torments."

"There is no greater torment, dear brother. We want to flee. All of us want to leave for America. But our country is a locked cage. And our friend holds the key."

"Which friend?" Father asked.

"Stalin, who else? You slipped away from him just in time. But let me tell you what a nightmare it is. Yes, we will escape. But it is not as easy to escape as it once was. Perhaps one in a thousand can save themselves. But one must escape. I decided that our sons should go first. One day, party officials assembled them along with many others, young and old. A number of our family members were among them. They announced that on our part of the river that flows from the lake to the sea and on its tributaries, they were going to erect high dams and build hydroelectric stations. They have not yet begun to build the first hydroelectric station, which will be located not far from the border, but they have a name for it nonetheless. It is going to be called 'Light of the Party,' and the others they have planned will be named Stalin, Marx, and Engels."

Father was shocked. Was he telling the truth? Was this possible? Had things come to such a pass? Guri Poradeci sensed Father's surprise, and he continued.

"Oh, those poor people want to construct hydroelectric stations. It is good for us to have light and more light, but what will we illuminate? Not a single road worthy of the name has been built since the Turkish era. We need a network of roads to join us, as we should be joined. But what they are doing is pulling us apart. If you want to travel from your village to a city you now need a permit. And for the first time in history, the party is gathering everyone from city and village, young and old, to train us, to turn us into the 'New

Man,' as they say. All this is to be accomplished through the construction of hydroelectric stations. That, my friend, is what the party has ordered. But life demands something else. They rounded up young and old, prisoners, 'enemies of the state,' traitors of the people, but most of all young people who had attempted to cross the border, my sons included."

It was now clear to Father what was on Guri Poradeci's mind.

"My sons have decided to escape," his friend continued his confession. "That is what we concluded the night their mother and I were last together with them. They have decided to flee to America. I said, 'whatever happens, happens.' We agreed. A mother is a mother; it was not easy for her to agree. But it would have been more difficult for them to stay and be conscripted for the construction of the hydroelectric stations. Attempts to flee across the border usually end in death. It was easier before. You crossed the border at night in a boat and you landed in a different country. Now times are different. It seems that even the fish are stopped at the border. As for the people, what chance do they have?"

Father could not help thinking about the path of the eels. After all, he had had the same thought, to leave with his family for America before they blocked the path of the eels, hoping someday to *return*. Now it was becoming clear that Father and his friend were connected by the same dream of departure, each for his own reasons. But there was no way for the dream to be realized.

"We are going to leave, my friend," continued Guri Poradeci, "because what remains of our life is to flee. I duped that devil guarding the border and left the country to come here to see you. What advice can you give us? What path should we follow? North or east? Across the lake or the sea? We will stay behind so that our children can get out first. If they cross the lake and God helps them to reach you, please take them in."

"My friend, of course we will take them in," answered Father.

Still, Father did not know what to tell him, which direction his children should take. Although he was deeply immersed in thoughts — both physical and metaphysical — of following the path of the eels, he was unable to show Guri Poradeci and his sons a true path, a way across the border and across the other borders to reach America.

"It is an terrible misfortune to have to abandon one's native land," Father said pensively. "It is a greater misfortune, my friend, when you remain in your native land and they take away all your hope. Our hope lies in departure. That is our salvation."

Here their concepts of departure as a means of salvation became intertwined. While Father's hope of continuing, of following the path of the eels, was fading — disappearing below his horizon, quietly setting — for Guri Poradeci and his sons, that hope was just dawning.

Until hints of the blue dawn began to rise over the river, thoughts of his own departure and that of his friend tormented Father. One of them had come halfway, with no hope of continuing; the other had not begun the journey, but had faith to persevere until the end.

Chapter 29

The sun was rising on the happiest week in our exile. Mother, accustomed to getting up early, had begun her day even earlier than usual. The house already breathed the clean, dewy smell of the freshly watered flowers, whose aroma wafted up to the balcony. Mother had also risen early to mix the dough to bake the *pogacha*, as if today were a holiday.

Father's dear friend met all of us on the balcony, its windows wide open. It seemed to us that the water in the river was coursing faster than on other days. Gulls that had flown in across the southern, closed border were landing on the small island in the middle of the river. We sat down on the *minder* next to Father's friend.

"Ah, here you are, my young lads. Are you ready for a journey in the old boat?" he joked with us.

He had guessed our thoughts, which was not difficult. He promised that he would tell us about our family boat and about his *return* to our native land after leaving us on the other shore.

"Last call, my brave lads, for the boat journey across the lake!" he called out.

We had long been ready for this return trip from exile, ever since the day that we arrived on the opposite shore, and our family friend went back to where we had been.

"When I left you on the other shore, my soul was aching. I wasn't afraid for myself that I had to cross the border in the early dawn and leave the boat in its old place."

Our friend helped himself to a spoonful of preserves and drank the cold water that Mother had served him; then he continued.

"While I rowed back across to the shore where we had begun our journey, everything was quiet. I crossed the border almost without rowing. The boat seemed to move by itself. The patrol did not meet me. I rowed up to our house. It alone had lights on in the dead of night. I set the boat in its place. I tied it to the stake on the shore. I looked at it as if looking at a true friend who had successfully completed a mission. I tapped the oars lightly on its side in a friendly way."

"Your mother sensed my presence," continued our family friend, turning to Father. "She had not closed her eyes. Your sisters and other members of the family were there. I told them that I had successfully brought you to the other shore of the lake. Other relatives arrived. Not content with the bare facts, they begged for more, for more than what had actually happened.

"They asked me for days, for months, for years to retell the short history in greater detail, in greater depth of how you crossed to the other shore. It ended up being another story altogether, a longer, more detailed one. Your mother, poor thing, would often go to the boat, to feel your absent proximity. Your poor mother."

That is how we learned the story of our crossing, how we were separated from our close family when Father's dear friend, his blood brother, brought us in the boat to our new country. Now here he was, our savior, herald of our fate, presenting us an eel, and prepared to give to those of us on this side of the border the details of our lost time.

"What happened with the boat, with *our* boat? Is it still alive?" we children asked.

"The boat, ah, the boat…as long as the occupation lasted, members of the family who were still there used it, but then after the war — "

"What happened to the boat after the war," my oldest brother asked impatiently.

"Right away, terrible things happened."

Silence descended. We already knew what kinds of misfortunes had occurred; the weight of those misfortunes had been borne on the backs of many in the family. In the context of these misfortunes, we did not want to repeat our question about the fate of our boat. It would have been too much. Quiet set in. Our father's friend spoke again.

"What are you thinking about? You must be dying to know what happened to the boat?"

"Of course, of course!" we all shouted.

"As the war ended, the hunt for enemies began. Most horrific was that people were pitted against their own families. But let us not talk about that."

Father's friend moved away from that theme again.

"Eventually," he continued, "they remembered that you had left. It was not difficult to dream up charges. Everything was rigged. Over time, they would select the guilty parties. Anyone could be accused of anything. Those were dark days. They took from you whatever you had: your house, your field, your vineyard, your mill. They finally got around to directing their attention to the old boat. They asked, 'Whose boat is this? How did you end up owning a family boat?' Fortunately, no one whispered that I had brought you across the lake, across the border. That was a miracle. I would have suffered for it."

Did they need to be told that the boat was a great bridge of goodness that connected shores and people in difficult times! How many soldiers and conquerors had the boat endured, always obedient, always ready for new travels?

"But is our boat still alive?" we asked, again interrupting Father's friend.

"I will tell you, I will tell you everything, but in order," he continued. "For a long time, the boat sat alone, tied up on the shore, always ready for an unexpected voyage. No one thought to move it from its place. It had stood at its mooring for a hundred years. Since the Ottoman era. It took care of itself; it was like a part of the lake. No one thought of stealing it. They knew that at some point, they might need it.

"But one day, the regime took control of the boat. It was to be collectivized. They did it by force. Just as people were being pushed into 'voluntary' labor collectives, the boat was to become part of the collective fishing 'fleet.' They decided to adapt it to the new era. They even painted it red, and on the bow they drew a five-pointed star and a hammer and sickle.

"They struggled quite a bit to change the appearance of your old boat. But the boat wasn't like the others. It had been built with care and know-how. Repairs had been done whenever they were needed after long use. Nothing gets accomplished by force. One night, after it had been altered, the boat disappeared."

"Where did it disappear to?" we asked at once.

"No one ever figured out whether it was carried off by the wind, or whether it was something else. Perhaps someone rowed off without being seen; it was visible far from shore, just about in the middle of the lake, and then it sank. People from the fishermen's collective began a search for it along the shore, but your boat was never found."

We listened sadly to what Father's friend told us about the disappearance of our boat; we younger children listened with tears in our eyes. For years, we had sailed in our imaginations back across the lake in our boat. We crossed the border; we reached the harbor beside the home of our birth. We had inherited Father's dream that one day, the old boat that brought us would take us back, and we would remain on the lake's other shore. It circled back and forth in our dreams. Now we were one illusion poorer. One less dream. As captain of a lost ship, our old family friend Guri Poradeci comforted us, saying that old boats, like people, disappear when their time has come.

At dawn, the day of separation arrived. Guri Poradeci left, crossing the threshold as if stepping into legend, so uncertain was the possibility of his ever returning. We all hugged him in turn, as if he were our lost country, a country we had discovered again that was now distancing itself from us forever. Then he set off along the river. We could see him clearly until he reached the solitary wooden bridge. There he disappeared from view. He was lost to us forever. We never saw him again.

After his departure, dark times took hold in the Balkans once again. As people reached the depths of misfortune, the leaders of the countries reinforced the borders. They kept dividing the people. And this was the cursed moment when the path of the eels was stopped.

When Guri Poradeci crossed the border, at the time he left us, crossing was still possible to imagine. Later, not even imagining was possible. The border rose, part of the Great Balkan Wall. Not even birds could fly over it. The only certainty was that the eels in the rivers could still freely cross the border on their long path to the ocean and back. Though not for long. Their freedom had been enough for Father not to give up his search for an exit that might allow him travel the path of the eels through his native land. But this hope grew smaller and smaller.

As for us children, we continued in our dreams to search every possible harbor for our lost boat. While the old captain returned to the eternal lake, we searched for a possible route toward the path of eels, to reach America either ahead of them or behind them. Each was left to his own fortune.

Chapter 30

Many years have passed since our old friend brought an eel and a trout to our family along with the breath of our native land. His visit upset our life as immigrants as never before. It challenged our thinking along the two constant poles of exile: to stay or to go — with the hope of one day returning to the place where we had begun, the point from which we had betrayed our native land.

Life in the house by the river — a way station on the path of our endless exile — carried us along as we hoped in vain to set off again someday to discover our family's lost Atlantis. The feeling never left us that we had to live a different life, one far removed from the one we had lived before. But in a foreign land, days melted quickly away. We barely sensed our youth passing by.

Time passed slowly after Guri Poradeci's departure. No one came from across the border. Fewer and fewer people emigrated, only a small number who fled in secret to continue on toward distant continents, only the bravest, willing to risk in advance their own lives in their attempt to cross the border. And so the borders grew stronger, they increased; the Balkan labyrinth grew tighter. In Father, the idea of possible escape was slowly dying. The Balkan wall rose higher, and people's spirits grew ever more desolate. The border even cut time in two; there was no news, neither of the living nor of the dead.

At this time, Father slowly lost interest in the eels and their path. He was, however, still obsessed more generally with the migrations of all living things on the planet. The ultimate goal of his search, one that would bring forth his own cry of eureka, was still to discover parallels between pathways of human migration and the migration pathways of all other living creatures.

He was consumed by his quest, seeking out the differences between natural phenomena and deviations in the natural order most often caused by man, who claimed that such actions were justified by loftier goals. Father concluded that human beings would travel along the cursed pathways of history, fatally distancing themselves from their own nature. Caught up in such thoughts, Father began, for the who-knows-what time, to reorder his library. Mother used to become anxious when Father shifted directions, but she had grown accustomed to it over time.

It seemed that Father, as he sought some way out of the Balkan labyrinth, struggled more than at any previous time with the ordering of his library. He still kept close at hand his books about human migration and the migrations of other living things, especially the migration paths of eels, which continued to foster his illusions of departure, his hope that he could follow their path. That path was becoming increasingly difficult. Still, why not keep those books close by?

Books about goats began to occupy an increasingly prominent place in his library; books about eels did not press so tightly against them. This was clear evidence that Father was becoming more engaged with the family's current circumstances — this was a time when villagers were prohibited from raising goats so they could form a powerful urban working class that would drive progress to catch up with the West — and he began distancing himself yet further from his utopian idea of following the path of the eels.

The holy books continued to stand on the upper shelf; just below them were Father's books about Janissaries, which he believed contained the most complex ideas for understanding Balkan history. Books about the Janissaries held their central position in his library to the end of his life. They were a part of Father's daily reading; they provoked his thoughts connected with his study of the history of the Balkans through the collapse of the three dominant Empires — the Roman, the Byzantine, and the Ottoman — through whose ruins the fates of the Balkan nations had been dragged.

With time, Father's library became a true Balkan Tower of Babel out of which he built an inventory of the main ideas for finding a natural exit from the rapid flow of history. It was as if Father wanted to take hold of the entirety of Balkan history, to tame it, to pull it all together through the most significant books, to make it as understandable as possible. But there was nothing more unstable, murkier, more puzzling, more amenable to multiple interpretations than what had been written about Balkan history, a history extolled by new writers — the victors who almost never connected their history with what had come before, but always began anew. History should begin with them. That is why Father's project, the *History of the Balkans through the Collapse of Its Empires*, had to begin with the stories of those who had been defeated.

But who could understand why, in those difficult, barbaric times marked by the beating of drums and slogans about progress and making up for lost time, a time of revolutionary songs about the working class, Father began to read books about labyrinths? It took years to uncover the metaphor Father revealed through those books.

In the end, the library itself had become a labyrinth with many intersections; there were more overlapping themes than books ordered by a single classification. The library was ordered by Father's unique system, one that would lead to our escape. No exit from the labyrinth had been found in the march of progress. The forward march did not bring escape from the labyrinth any closer. An exit could also be found by turning back. Other ideas arose as well whenever there was a change in the order of Father's books.

As a family, we were accustomed to the occasional tremors that came from Father's library, especially before we were to move again. They were harbingers of our migrations. But the search for the path of the eels along the river from where it flowed from lake, then across the sea, the ocean, and back, and the similarities with our emigrant saga combined with a turning point in Father's life, one that to a large extent altered our family's fate. It was Father's discovery of an old qadi's court records, a discovery of a lost Ottoman era. For Father, this was the discovery of a true written account of a Balkan Atlantis, of an era that had been severed and lost, which he believed would lead to a new understanding in the Balkan peoples of the complexity of their identity — and to a new discovery of their history.

Once again, a connection was being made in Father's mind between the discovery of his Atlantis of manuscripts and the severing of the path of the eels—though it was one that was, in the end, fully apparent to him alone. He sensed that these Ottoman manuscripts, these court records, preserved much of Balkan time. Often, while absorbed in the yellowed, ancient pages of the unbound court registers that had almost completely crumbled to dust, Father, by simply turning a sheet of paper, would provoke a prolonged rustling, freeing a voice of the life enclosed within, which could, in turn, link to voices enclosed in other pages within the loose pile of manuscripts.

Those yellowed papers scattered about Father's library were not ordinary papers eaten away by time. They were the lives of countless people: families, generations, clans, nations. They were signs of a life that had been consigned to oblivion. Countless signs emanating from dead souls.

Father believed that a sign from those court documents could be resurrected in the souls of those who had heretofore been unable to grasp the fullness of their identity. The signs struggled on the paper that time had eroded, the last signs of a way of life that had disappeared, to pass on their last messages as inspiration to their descendants.

It was for Father to assemble them, interpret them, give them meaning, accord them significance, and bring them to life. In this way, he would inspire many to search the clear breaks in their family's continuity. During the block of Ottoman time, everything had become intertwined, intermixed, and nearly lost forever. Just as at one time, when he had found himself in the graveyard of the Eyüp mosque in Constantinople, confronted by the headstones — endless exclamation marks and question marks, lives lived — he had been overcome by a melancholic sadness because he had been unable to find his mother's close relations, of whom he had no knowledge. He was happy that in these pages, before they vanished forever, he would be able to discover the messages of forgotten generations, connecting them with future generations.

Father deeply believed that, in searching through these court records, he would reach the very core of the broken family continuity — from his mother's family, the qadi's family, who had at one time lived in this land of his exile. He hoped that within these pages he would reach the muffled voices of his ancestors. Father threw himself into this search. From time to time, he spoke to those ancestors out loud. He strained to find a pathway to them. He calmly turned over the pages in the yellowed records one by one, stopping where a page had been eaten by time, its meaning lost.

He paused to interpret the break, as if searching for segments of lost time, as though together they could create a map that would retrace the family's history. He searched the old lettered pages as he once searched his books about eels — which had not revealed to him the fullness and salvation he had envisioned for his family — and through all this, he still never abandoned the eels completely; when he became disheartened by his search through the old Ottoman court records, Father would turn once again to his notes about the eels.

Epilogue

Father knew that a real exit from the Balkans would remain impossible for many more years. The network of borders across the Balkan landscape would be long maintained. But the books, each book in Father's library, signified a new voyage coursing down the great river of his life, meandering through all its twists and turns. Father's quest to find the path of the eels was, in the end, a metaphysical one. In his metaphorical search at the end of his life, he imagined himself as Zarathustra, the wanderer, who said, "I stand now before my last summit and before that which hath been longest reserved for me. Ah, my hardest path must I ascend! Ah, I have begun my lonesomest wandering!"

Father, in the end, sought a path that did not exist. In his search for that unattainable *somewhere*, the goal was not to reach a specific place; it was the search within him that was important, to find the essence of his identity amid the crossroads of his soul.

The mythic expanse of the lake spread deep in the family psyche; it possessed each of us in a special way. To Father, it was clear that there, within the expanse of quiet blue waters, were written the invisible archetypal contours outlining our family history. Here one could feel the source of the power of nature and follow the path of the eels, the most unusual pathway on the planet. Here, at the very springs of the great blue lake, the family was destined to inherit the endless dream of continuing life in exile, a dream that had begun by the seaside. We had come to live by these water sources following the great battle of life and death, following the great division when part of our family, our people, set off across the sea, others toward dry land. The two pathways of travel never ended. We never again saw those who had gone across the sea.

The belief remained that only by following the path of the eels would it be possible to accomplish a *return* to the places from where they had departed. We intensely believed that someday, following a watery course, we would rejoin those who had long ago departed, and together we would seek our path of *return*.

***

For a long time, Father was caught between his search for the path of the eels — that happy, symphonic planetary fugue that forged an eternal and happy link between the Balkans and the world — and his search through the old Ottoman qadi's documents, the *sicili*, or court records, Balkan documents that hid the riddle of the family's identity and the idea of maintaining hope for a rapid return to our native home by the lake.

Events unfolded, for the most part, as Father had predicted. While Stalinism declined in this country bordering the lake, particularly after the historic fight between Tito and Stalin, the spirit of Stalinism did not fully fade away. To tell the truth, construction did not begin on dams and hydroelectric plants during the Stalinist era, a time when Father, anticipating the severing of the path of the eels, took his family away from the town where the river flowed from the lake. It began ten years later.

Construction began on the first hydroelectric station near where the river flowed from the lake the year of the largest earthquake in the history of the Balkans, in the capital city of the Republic. First, the direction of the river's current was reversed, and then, when construction work was completed two years later, it was blocked completely. Several years later, a second dam, with still higher embankments and a larger hydroelectric station, was built right at the border.

News came from the other side of the border, from Albania, that there, too, dams and hydroelectric stations were being built, just as Guri Poradeci told Father they had been. One hydroelectric station after another was built with the names "Light of the Party," "Stalin," "Marx–Engels." Even if Father could understand the construction of the hydroelectric stations on the river in his native country, Albania, where Stalinism still ruled, he could not understand why, in the country that had been freed of Stalinism and was open to the world, the path of the eels had been severed in such brutal fashion.

But what happened to the poor eels? Were they forgotten forever? The last generation of eels to succeed in crossing unimpeded from the lake through the river to the sea and out to the ocean before the river was blocked returned through their descendants and was stopped by a new Balkan wall. And there were thousands, millions of eels. Nearly all of them perished, many ground up in the turbines. There was a true massacre of the eels.

During the time of Little Eel Drimski and Sreten Javorov, when construction of hydroelectric stations on the river was anticipated, the question was raised concerning construction of parallel eel ladders. But that idea was abandoned as unprofitable. A different proposal from that time was carried out, namely, to maintain an eel population in the lake by introducing baby eels, foreign to this lake, from other water sources, eels with, of course, different genetic codes of return. But that is a different story of eels condemned to a lake prison, a labyrinth with no exit.

The eels experienced an opposite fate to that of the people. In those years, Balkan borders were opened, except those between our native land and the land in which we lived. People left the Balkans, but the eels were imprisoned in the lake forever.

Years passed. Father completely abandoned his obsession of following the path of the eels. Books about eels in his library were hidden by piles of other books and documents. Mother was happy in her own way that the subject had passed from his thoughts forever, or so it seemed.

Up until the very end of his life, Father devoted himself to the Ottoman court records. He was committed to following a different path, one that led to a less utopian horizon than that of the eels. The family ultimately dropped anchor in the city beside the fortress rising above the great river.

During those years, news also came from Guri Poradeci. His sons had managed to cross the border and set off on the path of the eels. They reached America, but the old family members remained forever in their native country. The sons went through difficult times before they reached far-off America; they passed through the immigrant's purgatory on the small island beside the Statue of Liberty. Eventually they became employed in business, with varying success; the youngest became a member of the crew on a spaceship that circled the planet Earth. But poor Guri Poradeci never saw his sons again.

***

Years have passed since the time of the building of the dams and hydroelectric stations on the river that flows between the two countries. Almost nothing remains of that former stormy time when the fate of the eels was discussed. Oblivion became stronger than anything. As the twentieth century ended, there were signs of new stormy times. The Balkan countries were freed from the confines of ideological totalitarianism; even, amazingly, in our native country, Stalinism fell. Huge monuments to Enver Hoxha and Stalin toppled.

Father, in his unfinished *History of the Balkans through the Collapse of Its Empires*, as much as he had desired this turnaround in his native land, had been unable to foresee it. He has not been with us for a long time. Mother's life, too, ended beside Father's books. Without their presence, the books do not radiate their former messages. But for us, those messages remain, sources for us to learn about the history of the Balkans and the people who have inhabited its cursed expanse.

For us children, Father's books have never disappeared. Father's library has not died. His books have not died. Nor has the shifting order of his once-upon-a-time reading of the books faded in our memories. In these books his time rests in peace. For many years after Father's departure, Mother remained the holy guardian of Father's library. Each of us children, at different periods in our lives, has had a vital part of that library, whatever part we believed held the secret of our exile from the Balkans, the code of return from exile, and the phoenix code of our survival.

The great secret of Father's life lay hidden in the books about eels. The books continued to live inside us, steps along our fate, whose significance never diminished. The recollection of Father's books also was important for our own pathways in life. We recalled the order of the books in his library at different phases of our exile. This even affected our choice of life profession. Father's books followed us in our lives. We were stronger with them; we could more easily overcome our exile. They defined our first pathways in life, our professions. We, together with our heirs, were forever marked by them. The oldest brother, no doubt, marked by Father's illusions that we follow the eels toward America to seek our exit route from the Balkans, became engaged in studying the construction of dams. He became a well-known hydro-engineer and both his son and daughter chose to study hydro-engineering. The next brother, enraptured by Father's books about goats and eels became a renowned zoologist, and his oldest son became a doctor, the younger son studied veterinary sciences. As it turned out, this son was the greatest carrier of Father's gene, marked for travel and for realizing the project to reach the shores of America like the eels. It turned out that Father's grandson did reach America. He carried out Father's will, and followed the eels on their path to America. This grandson won a reputation in his profession. He became director of a company that was to complete an American aid project for the control and enforcement of standards in food production in the Balkans during the transition period following the fall of Communism. The path of return led this grandson to Albania. Then, knowing the epic of the return of the eels, he wrote in a telegram to the narrator of this book: "A little eel has returned ... "

And thus, the circle of our family's flight into exile was marked at last by the return of our Eel to its native Albania. This occurred after the fall of Stalinist Communism in that country when the walls at the borders were destroyed. Then thousands of Albanians left the country in secret. First they overwhelmed the embassies, then they stormed the boats and crossed the Adriatic.

The history of their ancestors, who had fled with their old faith after five hundred years of Ottoman rule, was repeating. Now people were escaping, freed from this latest ideology, faith in Stalinist Communism. In a new way, history, the metaphoric history of the path of the eels, was repeating. Those who returned thought of reclaiming the path of the eels, moving backwards in history, while those who left were fleeing once again, seemingly frightened as if from some atavistic fear that led to flight. It was felt that only in flight could that fear disappear. This fear was the fear of themselves in encountering an unknown life in other lands. The cursed cycles of an exile's fate.

The passing of time brought other wonders. The saga of the Balkan eel rose again in the minds of Igor Lozinski's descendants. In the heated clash between Cvetan Gorski and Little Eel Drimski that took place in the town where the river flowed from lake, the former director named during the Stalinist era achieved a pyrrhic victory. The dams were built. Cvetan Gorski was left to take care of Igor Lozinski's collection of lake flora and fauna, with a special section devoted to the path of the eels, which had been turned into a beautiful and unique museum in that town by the river.

Toward the end of the twentieth century, a group of young scientists and university professors in Skopje, the capital city of the newly independent Republic of Macedonia created after the division of Yugoslavia, articulated anew the goal of rescuing the world's Balkan eels. They proposed a project to rejuvenate the path of the eels, which had been severed by the dams and hydroelectric stations along the river that flowed from the lake to the sea, a river that ran between two Balkan countries that were at times in conflict, at other times at peace, with borders that had been at first walled shut but then became so open that families on both sides were almost lulled into believing that they did not exist.

The young scientists' project received first prize from the Ford Foundation in far-off America. But their plan, despite its scientific merit, could not correct the earlier mistake of not building special eel ladders to save the path of the eels. Their project envisioned, in a kind of science fiction fantasy, a renewal of the path of the eels through openings in the high embankments and the construction of water lifts. These would have resolved the height differences and thus revived the path of the eels. It was almost unimaginable that the path of the eels could be revived in this way, but no one could stop these scientists from imagining that the path of the eels might be reopened.

The disruption of the path was, however, fatal. Even if the path of the eels had been opened in the way scientists had hoped, the eels' inherited code of return had been lost forever. Now, with a different genetic code of remembrance, it was uncertain how the eels would return to the lake. They remain lost in the Balkan labyrinth.

Struga, Paris, Skopje, 1994–2000

Acknowledgments

"The Eel" by Eugenio Montale and translated from the Italian by Millicent Bell was published here with permission of Millicent Bell and the editors of *AGNI*, vol. 51

The translator, Christina E. Kramer, would like to thank the National Endowment for the Arts for its support of her work in translating this book from Macedonian.